CINEMATIC DESTINIES

"Leavy's prose is fluid, warm, and often poetic, capturing both the beauty of everyday moments and the emotional complexity of her characters' inner lives . . . A gentle, heartfelt story of the messy beauty of becoming."
—*Kirkus Reviews*

"*Cinematic Destinies* is a stunning and poignant celebration of romance, the magic of movies, and life itself. The exotic Icelandic film set, well-drawn characters, and smart writing make this book impossible to put down. Leavy is a gifted writer who weaves beauty and hopefulness into each of her tales. This is a gorgeous novel."
—Laurel Richardson, author of *Lone Twin*

"Emotionally charged, beautifully written, and deeply satisfying, this is a book you don't want to miss."
—Jessica Smartt Gullion, author of *October Birds*

"*Cinematic Destinies* is a gorgeous celebration of love, art, and the true meaning of life. The characters will live in my heart forever. They remind us how art inspires life and life inspires art. This novel is a cozy love letter to love itself and a testament to all the beauty to be found by simply living to the fullest. I absolutely loved this book! Highly recommended!"
—Jessie Voigts, PhD, founder of Wandering Educators

"A tour de force! *Cinematic Destinies* is a romantic masterpiece. This book was so captivating that I read it in one sitting and cried happy tears for the last several chapters. I literally could not speak for hours. It was just so beautiful and emotionally satisfying."
—U. Melissa Anyiwo, editor of *Gender Warriors*

"This light-hearted new novel returns us to the story of Finn Forrester and Ella. We glimpse what 'happily ever after' has looked like in action for these two. How delightful to see this cozy family embracing vulnerability more courageously as their children mature—and accepting that sometimes a little trial and error imparts the best lesson of all!"
—Alexandra Nowakowski, coauthor of *Other People's Oysters*

"This novel will pull at heartstrings, open tear ducts, and produce laughs all at once!"
—J. E. Sumerau, 2021 George Garrett Fiction Prize winning author of *Transmission*

"Leavy's riveting story of what happens in the happily-ever-after shows us how the legacy of love and art are the greatest gift. We see how love can be complicated and messy but taking a chance on the one that makes your heart soar, especially when it frightens you, is an act that sheds light in the darkest places. I loved this book."
—Sandra L. Faulkner, author of *Poetic Inquiry: Craft, Method and Practice*

PRAISE FOR
AFTER THE RED CARPET

"A fun read from start to finish . . . a welcome and unreservedly recommended addition to the personal reading lists of dedicated romance fans."
—*Midwest Book Review*

"Leavy's writing shines in its ability to delve into the emotional intricacies of a relationship, offering readers a glimpse into the characters' heartfelt explorations of trust, understanding, and mutual support. This novel is an inviting read for those who appreciate a story that reaches the heights of romantic idealism and savors the everyday moments that weave two lives together."
—*Literary Titan*, 5-star review

"*After the Red Carpet* is a modern masterpiece and a perfect romance narrative from the more literary side of the book world."
—*Readers' Favorite*, 5-star review

"Overall, the book is a frothy, sunny read."
—*Kirkus Reviews*

PRAISE FOR
THE LOCATION SHOOT

"Each character is more charming than the next . . . the intellectual discussions throughout the book prove fresh and engaging and will keep the pages turning. A quick-witted depiction of moviemaking best suited for contemplative romantics."
—*Kirkus Reviews*

"Patricia Leavy's *The Location Shoot* is hard to put down. . . . Leavy is a master storyteller, skillfully weaving together a narrative that keeps us engaged from start to finish. . . . Ultimately, it's a must-read for anyone looking for a thought-provoking and entertaining exploration of love, relationships, and self-discovery. Highly recommended!"
—*Readers' Favorite*, 5-star review

"The narrative's charm isn't solely defined by the romantic entanglement of a central couple but also by its well-sketched ensemble cast."
—Literary Titan, 5-star review

"A tour de force! Much more than a romance, this novel celebrates the romance of life itself. Leavy's voice in fiction is singular. She brings her laser-like wit, intelligence, and hopefulness to this enchanting and truly unforgettable love story."
—Laurel Richardson, author of *Lone Twin*

PRAISE FOR
SHOOTING STARS ABOVE

"Patricia Leavy crafts a riveting narrative that shows the healing power of love and how it helps wounded souls become whole once again."

—*Readers' Favorite*, 5-star review

"The strongest book I've ever read . . . It gave me hope and made me remember why all kinds of love are worth fighting for."

—*The Book Revue*, 5-star review

PRAISE FOR
HOLLYLAND

"This quick read will leave readers satisfied with the happy ending. The main characters will make readers believe in love. Fans of Colleen Hoover and Tessa Bailey will enjoy *Hollyland*."

—*Booklist*

"Written with the kind of eloquence associated with award winning literary fiction . . . An impressively poignant, laudably original, and thoroughly entertaining novel that moves fluidly between romance, humor, suspense, and joy, *Hollyland* is one of those stories that will linger in the mind and memory long after the book itself has been finished and set back upon the shelf . . . highly recommended."

—*Midwest Book Review*

CINEMATIC DESTINIES

CINEMATIC DESTINIES

A Novel

PATRICIA LEAVY

SHE WRITES PRESS

Copyright © 2025 Patricia Leavy

All rights reserved. No part of this publication may be reproduced, stored in a retrieval system, or transmitted in any form or by any means, electronic, mechanical, photocopying, recording, or otherwise, except for brief quotations in reviews, educational works, or other uses permitted by copyright law.

Published in 2025 by
She Writes Press, an imprint of The Stable Book Group

32 Court Street, Suite 2109
Brooklyn, NY 11201
https://shewritespress.com
Library of Congress Control Number: 2025909813
ISBN: 978-1-64742-948-5
eISBN: 978-1-64742-949-2

Interior Designer: Tabitha Lahr

Printed in the United States

This is a work of fiction. Names, characters, places, and incidents are either products of the author's imagination or are used fictitiously. Any resemblance to actual persons, living or dead, is purely coincidental.

No part of this publication may be used to train generative artificial intelligence (AI) models. The publisher and author reserve all rights related to the use of this content in machine learning.

All company and product names mentioned in this book may be trademarks or registered trademarks of their respective owners. They are used for identification purposes only and do not imply endorsement or affiliation.

In memory of Mr. Barry Shuman

PROLOGUE

| May 25 | *Entertainment News Report* |

French filmmaker Jean Mercier's impending retirement has sent shock waves through the film industry. Known for tackling daring subjects with his avant-garde approach to cinema, the controversial filmmaker has long been considered one of the few true artists of contemporary film. Although retirement seems inevitable at the age of 89, many in the industry thought he'd die with a director's clapboard in his hands, a joke the eccentric artist has often made himself. The announcement comes one week before shooting is scheduled to begin on what we now know will be his final film. Mercier famously films in remote locations, living in seclusion with his lead actors in rented homes and inns. The award winner is known for curating unexpected casts, and his choices this time are sure to create a buzz.

Leading the cast is American actor Michael Hennesey, 69, who became widely known for his Emmy-winning role on *Desperation and Despair* before becoming a formidable presence on the silver screen. Hennesey previously appeared in Mercier's acclaimed film *Celebration* thirty years ago. This is the first time the pair has reunited professionally.

British actor of stage and screen Rupert Reed, 29, is also set to star in the project. Reed is the son of playwright George Reed and actress Charlotte Reed. Charlotte Reed also starred in Mercier's film *Celebration*.

Finally, up-and-coming American actress Georgia Sinclair Forrester, 25, will appear in the unnamed film. Forrester is the middle child of Hollywood movie star Finn Forrester and provocative philosopher Gabriella Sinclair Forrester. Georgia is the only of the pair's children to follow in her father's footsteps. Eldest daughter Betty, 28, is in a medical residency program in New York, and their son Albert, 22, recently graduated from Boston University with an art degree. Fans will recall that Forrester and Sinclair met on the set of *Celebration*, for which Forrester won the Oscar. One of the most enduring marriages in Hollywood, the world has been captivated by their fairy-tale romance since Forrester proposed to Sinclair on the red carpet at the Cannes Film Festival.

So, it appears that Mercier is creating a family affair of sorts for his final picture. Is it nostalgia? Genius casting? Publicity? An attempt to reclaim the magic of his glory days? The world will be waiting to see.

CHAPTER 1

"Ella, where are you?" Finn called.
"Georgia's room."

Finn bounded upstairs and found Ella standing in a flowing yellow sundress, arranging a bouquet of colorful wildflowers. He came up behind her, slipped one hand around her waist, and moved her long spiral curls over before planting a delicate kiss on her shoulder. "Hi, love," he whispered. "Those are pretty."

"Wildflowers for Georgia, white roses for Betty, and daisies for our sweet Albert," she said. "I know it's only a long weekend, but I'm so excited they're all coming. We're hardly together as a family anymore. They'll all be busy over the summer, and who knows when we'll be together again. So, I wanted to make things special."

"Come here," he said, turning her to face him. "You always make everything special." He ran his finger along her hairline and kissed her softly.

"I worry about them, you know," she said.

"Why, love? They're all fine."

"Betty works such long hours. Seems she's always at the hospital and she only ever mentions one friend. I don't think she dates at all. Must be lonely in New York City on her own." Ella stopped and shook her head. "When she was little, she always looked out for her siblings and other younger children. Now she spends all her time taking care of others, and I worry about who will take care of her."

"She used to be such a romantic at heart. Don't you remember how obsessed she was with fairy-tale movies and stories? She'd refuse to leave the house without her wand and tiara."

"And the princess dresses. Heavens, she would throw a fit if I wouldn't let her wear one. And now . . ."

"Now?" Finn asked.

"It's like she's lost that part of herself, her romantic nature. She's become so serious. All work and no play."

"Medical school was a huge undertaking. Now she's dealing with the demands of her residency, but eventually she'll make time for other things," he assured her.

"Finn, do you really think life just waits for us? Love is inconvenient. It doesn't oblige our schedules. It requires an open heart and I'm just not sure if . . ."

"Hey," he whispered, stroking her cheek. "She'll find her way."

"I worry about Albert too. My shy, quiet, gentle Albert. He must get lonely, all the way on the other side of the country. We've always been so close, but lately when we FaceTime, I can't tell if he's happy. I look into his soft blue eyes and . . ." She trailed off.

"He's just a late bloomer. I know you were hoping he'd move back home after school, but going to Boston was good for him. The animation classes he's taking this summer along with his art degree will open a lot of doors. It's good for him to explore different ways to use his talent. More importantly, he's finding out who he is."

"I hope so." She glanced over at the vase. "Then there's our little wildflower, Georgia. She spends her life flitting from one place to the next, no roots, no real home base, one casual lover after the other."

"Sounds like someone I know, my bohemian bride," he said with a chuckle.

"Don't start with that."

"Ella, you and Georgia have always been so much alike. It's why you're at odds sometimes. She inherited your sense of humor, free spirit, wanderlust. The universe was damn clear because she's even your spitting image."

"Don't blame me. You're the actor. She's following in your footsteps."

"Baby, she's just adventurous. That comes from you. It's one of the things I fell in love with. Remember in the beginning how afraid you were of truly giving yourself to me? You were terrified I'd try to tame you, when all I wanted in the world was to love you." Finn took her face in both his hands and leaned his forehead against hers, lingering for a long intimate moment. He pulled back and kissed her passionately, weaving his fingers into her hair. "That's still all I want, to love you," he whispered, nibbling on her earlobe.

Ella wrapped her arms around him and softly said, "Love me right now. Take me to our room."

BETTY WALKED INTO THE RESIDENTS' LOUNGE, chugging a bottle of water.

"Hey, you're still here?" Khalil asked, sitting up from the bench he was sprawled out on.

"The delivery took forever. I felt sorry for the mother. But when she held her newborn, she seemed to forget all about the labor," Betty replied, tossing her empty bottle in the recycling bin and opening her locker.

"Best part of OB-GYN, right? We get to be a part of a lot of happy endings," he said.

She smiled. "Or happy beginnings, really. What are you still doing here? Didn't your shift end hours ago?"

"Oh, uh, just thought I'd stick around a bit," he stammered.

"Suit yourself," she said with a shrug.

Khalil watched as Betty stretched her arms, extending her tall, lean frame. She pulled the scrunchie out of her hair, releasing wavy blonde locks down to the middle of her back, and took a small roller suitcase out of her locker.

"You must be looking forward to seeing your family," he remarked.

She nodded. "My folks have been asking us to visit for so long. I feel bad because I do miss them, but you know what our lives are like. No time for anything."

"Yeah, we've really got to find a way to have a life," he muttered.

"Georgia's probably gonna be going on and on about her next film and whatever rando she's been sleeping with. She dates guys for like five minutes. Honestly, I don't see the point. I'd rather just be at home soaking in a warm bath doing a crossword." Khalil took a breath like he was going to respond, but she continued, "So, do you have big plans this weekend? Finally going to catch a Broadway play?"

He shook his head. "Doing a double. Figured without you here to kick my ass in Scrabble and overindulge on international takeout, I might as well get in the extra hours."

She smiled and started toward the door, wheeling her suitcase behind her.

"You're leaving straight from here?" he asked.

"Uh-huh. I brought my stuff just in case. Figured I might not have time to go home," she replied.

"Don't you want to change into street clothes?"

"No time," Betty said. "My dad sent his jet, and I'm already barely going to make the departure time. We're stopping in Boston on the way to LA to pick up my brother, so I can't be late."

"Well, if anyone can rock blue scrubs and black clogs, it's you," Khalil said.

She laughed. "It wouldn't faze them, they're used to me, but I'll change on the jet."

"Have a nice weekend."

"You too."

"Betty," he called, before she made it out the door. She turned to face him and raised her eyebrows. "When you get back, Scrabble and takeout? We could try that new Indian place."

"Sure," she replied. "Sounds great. Bye."

"Bye."

ALBERT SCOOPED UP HIS NOTEBOOKS AND colored pencils and stuck them in his laptop bag.

"Don't forget your headphones. For the plane," Ryan said, gesturing to the table.

"Thanks," Albert replied, sticking the headphones in the side pouch of his suitcase. "Listen, I gotta go. My ride's outside."

"Wait," Ryan said.

"My sister is pretty uptight. She'll be upset if I'm late for the flight."

"Please," he said, grazing Albert's hand and looking straight into his blue eyes. "Just sit with me for a minute. I'm sorry about last night and . . ."

"I really can't be late," Albert muttered, averting his gaze.

Ryan sighed. He extended his hand and implored, "Please, just give me a minute."

Albert reluctantly sat on the couch but kept his hands in his lap.

"What I said last night came out all wrong. I didn't mean it to sound like an ultimatum. But you've always said you're really close with your parents. Your mother already knows, and you said she completely accepts you. If you'd only tell your father then . . ."

"You don't understand."

"Then explain it to me."

Albert ran his hand through his sideswept ash-brown hair and took a deep breath. "My dad's a movie star, a leading man. And . . . he and my mom have this iconic love story. He proposed to her in front of the whole world, like it was nothing. They even named me after Albie Hughes, you know, the famous actor, and . . ."

"What?" Ryan asked.

"I don't want to disappoint anyone, that's all. I'm different from them and maybe I just want to fit in."

"Can't you fit in being yourself?"

"I'm . . . I'm not ready. I understand if you don't want to hang out anymore. Please lock up when you go back to your place. I'm sorry, I have to go," he said, rising. He opened the apartment door, and Ryan called to him.

"Al, you spend so much time drawing superheroes. Maybe it's time to be the hero of your own story. You deserve that. You deserve to be who you are. We all do."

"Yeah," he whispered, gently closing the door behind him.

"FUCK, WHERE'S MY OTHER SHOE?" Georgia yelped, searching the floor, wearing only a G-string.

"Come back to bed, baby."

"I can't," she said, looking under the couch.

"You've got a great ass. Bring it back over here."

"Ah, here it is!" she exclaimed, holding up the brown leather sandal. "For a minute I thought I'd have to drive all the way to LA barefoot."

She stepped into the sandals and slipped her short sundress over her head, her long light brown spiral curls flowing freely down her back.

"Oh, come on, baby. Don't cover up that smoking bod. Just one more round."

"Can't," she said, leaning down to give him a quick smooch. "My folks are expecting me. They all think I'm flighty as it is. My siblings are traveling from across the country, so if I'm the one who's late, well, pretty much proves their point."

"What if I promise to make you squeal?" he teased, extending his tattooed arms.

"Sorry, but I gotta bolt," Georgia said with a giggle, leaning down again to give him one more peck. She ran her finger above the piercing over his eyebrow and said, "Have a great summer. Good luck with your band."

"Wait. When will you be back in San Fran?"

She shrugged. "I don't know, like maybe never. After LA I'll be abroad for the summer making a movie. Then, who knows. Maybe I'll go to New York to do theater again. Or maybe I'll take a break. I'd love to live in Tahiti or somewhere tropical for a while."

"You know where to find me," he said with a devilish glint in his eyes.

She smiled, revealing the dimples in her heart-shaped face, grabbed her slouchy hobo bag, and left.

"THAT WAS AMAZING," FINN WHISPERED, rolling beside Ella, his body still trembling. He gently swept his fingers from her brow to her cheekbone. "You are so beautiful. When

I look into those piercing green eyes, I don't ever want to look away."

"You're the most handsome man I've ever seen, my love," she said, kissing him softly.

"I'm an old man," he said with a chuckle. "I'm lucky you still want me."

"You just get sexier and sexier," she insisted, running her fingers through his salt-and-pepper hair and across the lines fanning out from his sea-colored eyes. "You are my everything, now and forever."

"And you're mine," he whispered, squeezing her shoulder and planting a tiny kiss on the tip of her nose. He stared adoringly at her as if searching for the words to express how he was feeling, and eventually said, "Marry me, Ella."

She giggled and said, "Maybe you're getting senile after all. We're already married."

Finn laughed. "Our thirtieth anniversary is coming up this fall. Let's renew our vows. There's nothing that would make me happier than marrying you again. Say yes."

"Yes," she said, smiling brightly. She lifted his hand and sprinkled little kisses on his fingers.

He pulled her closer and she settled against him. "I know you always worry about when we can get the family together. We can tell the kids this weekend to mark their calendars. Just an intimate celebration of our life and love, here in our home, where we got married."

"That sounds perfect," Ella said. She smiled, but it quickly evaporated, and her gaze fell downward. "I just wish . . ."

He lifted her chin until her eyes met his. "What is it, love?"

"The children. I want them to have all that life has to offer. To live and love with gusto. Like we've tried to do, but each in their own way."

"I want that too."

"I know you don't think I should worry . . ."

"You're an extraordinary mother. I love how you know them, how you look out for them. But we have to trust the job we did. They're okay."

"I hope so."

"All we can do is live and love with everything we have. Allow them to see the example we set."

"Sometimes I think their choices reflect their desire to be different from us, no matter the cost. Especially Georgia. She worships you, but . . ."

"Hey," Finn said, caressing her shoulder. "She loves you fiercely. It's just that you're so much alike, whether you two see it or not, and she craves independence. Autonomy."

Ella sighed.

"Come here," he said, guiding her head to his chest and wrapping her in his strong arms. "Right now, just be with me."

"Always, my love."

CHAPTER 2

"Mom, how long are you going to hug me for?" Albert said.

"Just a minute more," Ella whispered as she held him tightly.

"Let the poor kid go," Finn joked, standing beside Betty.

Eventually Ella let go, rubbed Albert's arms, and smiled. "I'm just so happy you're home, that you're both home. Why don't you get settled and then come hang out by the pool? We're planning a barbecue out back when your sister arrives."

"Georgia's not here yet?" Betty asked.

"You know how she is. With any luck she'll make her grand entrance early enough that we can eat before midnight," Ella replied with a wink.

Betty laughed.

"I'm a little tired. Do you mind if I just chill in my room until dinner?" Albert asked.

"Sure, sweetheart. We'll be out back if you change your mind," Ella replied.

Albert picked up his suitcase and shuffled upstairs.

Ella slung her arm around Betty and asked, "Is everything okay with your brother?"

Betty shrugged. "He was quiet on the jet. Just drawing and listening to music with his headphones. You know how he is. I'm sure he's fine."

"Well, I wish he'd hang out with us, but this gives us a chance to catch up. We want to hear everything about your residency program and life in the Big Apple."

"We sure do," Finn added. "I'll bring your bag upstairs. Then we want to hear our girl tell us all about being a brilliant doctor."

Betty giggled. "I'm not brilliant."

"Yes, you are," Finn countered.

"Come on, no point in arguing," Ella said, giving Betty's shoulder a squeeze. "Let's go relax outside. I made lavender lemonade and your favorite snacks. We want to hear everything before Georgia gets here and commands the floor."

AS DUSK SET IN, ELLA AND FINN WERE rapt listening to Betty tell them stories about her residency program.

"When the second twin was finally born, we all breathed a sigh of relief," she explained.

"I bet," Finn said, beaming.

"What?" she asked.

"We're just so unbelievably proud of you," he replied.

"We sure are," Ella added.

Betty looked down, her fair cheeks turning rosy.

"Seems obstetrics was the right choice for you," Finn remarked.

"Yeah. It's unpredictable with crazy hours, and it's heartbreaking when things don't go well, so you have to really shut off your emotions. That's what it takes to do it well. To be a good doctor. You can't allow yourself to feel it." Ella glanced at Finn and Betty continued, "But most of the time, it's the best job in the world. There's nothing like helping deliver babies. It's incredibly . . ." She trailed off, as if trying to find the perfect word.

"What?" Ella asked.

"Hopeful. It's incredibly hopeful," Betty said, picking up her water glass.

Ella and Finn exchanged a smile and Betty continued, "Sometimes I have to remind myself that I have a job to do, and when it's over, I've done my part. On to the next. It's not like I get to see the children's lives." She stopped to take a sip of her drink before adding, "Who they become as adults."

"Oh, I don't know," Ella mused. "I think you can tell a lot from how we come into this world. Let's take you and your siblings. Heavens, I was in labor with you forever, writhing around in pain. Now that I know you, it's clear you were just taking your time. You're always so thoughtful, careful, and you never leap before you look. I'm sure it's made you an extraordinary doctor." Betty looked down shyly and Ella continued, "Now Georgia, on the other hand, practically flew out of me. The doctor had to catch her like a football. It was quite the entrance."

"That it was," Finn added with a chuckle.

"Seems she couldn't wait to get the hell out of me and out into the world, and that certainly hasn't changed," Ella said with a laugh. "Finally, Albert. His labor was shorter than yours, longer than your sister's, but it was mild, peaceful. When he was born, that final push somehow lasted a moment longer than all the others. Like he was timid about joining us." She shook her head. "So you see, how we come into this world says a lot about who we are."

"So, I guess the moral of that story is that Georgia's always been destined for the spotlight," Betty said.

"Damn straight!" Georgia exclaimed, dramatically throwing her arms up in the air as she sprinted toward her family.

Everyone leapt up to greet her.

"Little peach, I missed you," Finn said, wrapping her in a bear hug.

"Me too, Dad."

"Hey, I want some of that," Ella said. The two embraced affectionately. "I missed you too, sweet girl."

"Me too, Mom."

Betty hugged Georgia and whispered, "Good to see you, drama queen."

"You too, brainiac," Georgia replied.

"So, we're glad you could join us before dark," Ella teased.

"I planned to be here hours ago, but I got lost leaving the Bay Area and then I had a problem with the stupid convertible sports car I rented. Long story, but I made it. Where's Al?"

"Resting in his room until dinner," Ella replied.

Georgia furrowed her brow. "I don't think so. I'll go drag his ass out. Back in a flash. You can talk about me while I'm gone," she said, darting off.

As soon as she was out of earshot, Finn, Ella, and Betty burst into laughter.

When the laughter died down, Ella smiled and said, "Georgia's home."

GEORGIA TAPPED ON THE DOOR BEFORE letting herself in. Albert was sitting on his bed with his headphones in his lap.

"Hey, snot face," she said, barreling over to him.

He beamed as she plopped down on the edge of his bed and leaned over for a big hug.

"So, what kind of sad stereotype is this?" she joked, gesturing at the headphones. "Don't tell me, you were listening to some indie band no one's ever heard of and contemplating the poetic futility of life. Step it up. Be more original. You're an artist for fuck's sake."

Albert laughed.

Georgia's expression turned more serious. "You know I'm just teasing. What gives? Why are you up here all alone?"

"I was just a little tired. Jet lag."

Georgia stared him down, silently prodding him to fess up. He sighed. "I was thinking, that's all. I just have some stuff on my mind. Personal stuff to figure out."

"Well, for what it's worth, my best advice is always the same. Be yourself because yourself is fabulous."

Albert smiled. "I'm so glad you're here. I missed you."

"Missed you more," she said, tousling his hair.

"Hey," he protested, fixing his hair.

"We better go. They're waiting for us. Don't worry, if you feel like being quiet, I'll cover for you. I have oodles to tell everyone about my new movie. Come on," she said, tugging his hand.

"DAD, DID YOU READ THE TRADES?" Georgia asked as she helped herself to a piece of grilled chicken.

"I did. You're making quite the splash, little peach," he replied.

She beamed. "Everyone's predicting this will be my big breakout role. That nothing will ever be the same again."

"You're very talented. Just remember what I've always told you, what Grandma used to tell me. Be truthful in your performances. People need their stories told. And never forget it's a privilege to be an artist." He glanced over at Albert and said, "That applies to you too, with your visual art. You're also very talented."

Albert smiled bashfully and Georgia jumped back in, "I know, Dad. I love getting lost in the stories."

"You're in for quite an education. Being in a Jean Mercier film is a singular experience. No one works the way he does.

Be prepared. No rehearsals, no blocking. Half the time, no damn clue what's going on," he said with a chuckle.

Georgia nodded. "I know. His style is legendary. I think it will be perfect for me. I never overprepare. I always try to find the moment. Let it happen naturally."

"He wouldn't have cast you if he didn't think you'd be exceptional. He's got a knack for these things. You'll grow a lot on this job. It will be good for you in more ways than you can imagine." Finn let out a puff and continued, "Hell, my first Mercier film changed my whole life. It's where I met your mother."

Finn and Ella stared at each other from opposite ends of the table.

"Uh, hello. Not to mention you snagged an Oscar," Georgia said.

Finn laughed. "Trust me, the gold I scored on that set was your mother."

"So true," Ella said matter-of-factly. She giggled in her husband's direction and then looked at Georgia and asked, "So, are you going to tell us what the film is about?"

"It's all top secret, so you have to promise not to say a word," Georgia instructed.

"It will be hard to resist calling the tabloids. You know, when I have time in between facilitating the miracle of life," Betty joked.

Albert laughed, covering his mouth.

Georgia stared her down.

"Just teasing. Scout's honor," Betty said.

Georgia rolled her eyes. "It's called *Beauty*. We're filming in a remote location in Iceland. The script is pretty sparse. Some kind of metaphor or something."

"Yeah, that's how Jean works," Finn remarked.

"Basically, two men fall in love with my character. An old guy, and one who's more my age," Georgia explained.

"Please tell me you don't have any sex scenes with Michael. I don't think I can handle it," Finn lamented.

"Dad!" Georgia whined.

"I'm serious," he said.

"Don't worry. Nothing like that," she assured him.

"He better not hit on you for real either," Finn added.

"Dad! Gross! He's old like you."

Finn and Ella burst into laughter.

"Yeah, well that may not stop him. When your mom and I met him on the set of *Celebration*, he was quite the player."

"Oh, don't listen to your father," Ella chimed in. "Michael has been blissfully married to Lauren almost as long as we've been together. He's also a friend. There are some lines he wouldn't cross."

"Your mother is right. Much bigger chance that Jean hits on you," Finn said.

"Ick! He's like two hundred!" Georgia wailed.

Ella laughed. "Age hasn't slowed him down one bit. His reputation with women is well-earned. I can speak from experience. After all, he tried to feel me up when we first met. Come to think of it, I was a bit younger than you at the time."

"Gross!" Georgia, Betty, and Albert moaned in unison.

Ella giggled. "Don't worry, Georgia. He thinks of you as a niece. We're just teasing. Well, mostly. Jean is one of my oldest and dearest friends. We adore each other."

"Someone please change the subject. I don't want to hear any more about how my boss tried to feel up Mom," Georgia whined.

"Fair enough," Finn said with a laugh. He turned to his son and asked, "Are you looking forward to the summer classes you'll be taking at MassArt?"

Albert took a sip of water and responded, "Yeah. Thanks for letting me do it. I know I could have gotten a job right after graduation, but . . ."

"Your mother and I are happy to support your continued education," Finn assured him.

"Of course we are," Ella concurred.

"You've always been so passionate about drawing. We thought you'd get a job as an illustrator or something. What made you interested in studying animation?" Finn asked.

"I figured this would give me more options to turn art into a career." Albert looked down and added, "If I develop skills in animation, I might be able to do something in the entertainment industry. Maybe work in television or film. Hollywood even."

Finn smiled. "It's smart to create options for yourself."

"Whatever you do, we couldn't be prouder, my sweet boy," Ella added, leaning over and patting his hand. "I know how you get lost in your art and studies, but make sure you leave time for a social life this summer. You're only young once. Have some fun too."

"Yeah," Albert muttered, picking up his fork and taking a bite of chicken.

"It always sounded like you had some good friends at school. Did they all leave after graduation or are some still in Boston?" Ella asked.

Albert swallowed the food in his mouth and replied, "I still have a few people. It's why I wanted to move to Harvard Square. My friends are in the same apartment building. I don't mind taking public transportation to school."

"Good," Ella said. She turned to Betty. "What about that nice friend of yours your father and I met last time we visited you in New York? Khalil? How is he? We thought he was lovely."

"He's fine. Working crazy hours like me. Honestly, he's a lifeline. If it weren't for him, I'd have no life at all. We play a lot of board games and eat a ton of takeout. It's nice to have someone to keep you company who understands the demands of the job, the insane hours. A few weeks ago, I got new curtains for my apartment, and he came over to help me hang them. We do stuff like that for each other. Since neither of us is from New York, it's good we have each other."

"Uh, he totally sounds like your boyfriend," Georgia said.

"He is *not* my boyfriend," Betty protested.

"Board games, takeout, hanging upholstery. It sounds boring and monotonous. From what I hear, that's a boyfriend," Georgia said.

Betty rolled her eyes. "What about you? Who's your latest boy toy?"

"No one, really. And they're not toys. They're definitely not boyfriends either. They're just *lovers*," Georgia replied with dramatic flair.

"Okay, that may be enough of that," Finn said, his face turning red.

Ella laughed. "Don't listen to your father. There's nothing wrong with talking about sex."

"This coming from the woman who wrote about vibrators, blow jobs, and orgasms," Betty said, rubbing her eyes. "Do you have any idea what that was like for us growing up?"

"You know, for an obstetrician, you have a surprisingly narrow view of sex," Ella quipped.

"That's because she and her boyfriend spend all their time playing board games," Georgia squealed.

"He's *not* my boyfriend," Betty repeated.

"Well, if you need sex tips, read Mom's books. Seems Dad is a lucky guy," Georgia joked.

They exploded with laughter.

Finn's cheeks were bright pink. He raised his glass and said, "It's so much fun having you all here. We love it so much that we want to do it again. Mark your calendars. Your mother and I have a big anniversary coming up on the first of October. To celebrate the occasion, and because I'd do it all again in a heartbeat," he said, staring at his beloved, "we're renewing our wedding vows. It's a very special day for us and we want you here. I'll take care of the arrangements." The kids nodded, and Finn continued, "Cheers to being together!"

"Cheers!"

A little while later, they were all in the kitchen cleaning up. Betty, Georgia, and Albert were wrapping the leftovers and putting them away while Finn and Ella finished the dishes. As Ella was drying the last dish, Finn came up behind her, slipped his hands around her waist, and kissed the back of her head. Ella turned toward him. He ran his finger down her cheek and she looked down. Finn whispered something to her. She giggled and skimmed her fingers along his temple, their eyes glued to each other, their faces barely centimeters apart.

"Someone should really tell them to get a room," Betty whispered to her siblings.

"They're so weird," Georgia whispered in return.

Albert smiled. "I think they're great."

CHAPTER 3

When they arrived home after taking the kids to the airport, Ella shuffled into the house, her shoulders slumped.

"Come here," Finn said, taking her hand and leading her into the living room. They curled up together on the couch. He kissed the side of her head. "I know it's hard for you when they leave. They'll be back before you know it."

"It just always makes me a bit blue, seeing them go. We had so much fun."

"I know, baby. But they're all off doing such amazing things this summer. Betty is really shining in her residency program. I'm so proud of her. Oh, did Albert show you his latest drawings? They're amazing. He's so talented."

"Yes, he is. Artistic just like his father. You used to portray superheroes, and now he's creating new ones. Funny how that happens."

Finn gave her a gentle squeeze. "I still can't believe Georgia is starring in one of Jean's films. His last, I gather. There's something so profoundly full circle about it. It's had me thinking about when we filmed *Celebration*. You know, when we started shooting, Albie was the age I am now."

"Huh. I hadn't thought of that."

"Don't get me wrong. Albie was incredible. Such a skilled performer, and he lived to the fullest, but he struck me as an old guy." He stopped to chuckle. "Now I'm an old guy."

Ella looked into his eyes and caressed his cheek. "No, my love. People wear their age differently. Albie had a rough upbringing and abused alcohol for decades. By that summer he had also been sick on and off for years. It showed. It all aged him beyond his years. You are still so handsome, vibrant, and strong," she said, rubbing his biceps. "You were my superhero then as you are now. And forever. Hollywood agrees, because you're still a leading man too."

He kissed her forehead. "I have a confession to make, but I didn't want to say anything when the kids were here."

She raised her eyebrows.

"I called Jean a few days ago. I thanked him for casting Georgia and asked him to keep an eye on her this summer."

"You're a good father."

"He told me something that surprised me."

"Don't tell me he's getting married again? Let me guess, wife number four is barely old enough to drink."

Finn laughed. "No, he told me that he had tried to cast *you* in a film, back when you first met, when you were in your twenties. He said he begged and pleaded, but you weren't interested. I knew when you and Jean met, he invited you to tag along on a location shoot in Barcelona, but not that he wanted you in the film."

"The whole thing was so absurd. I wasn't an actress. That was just Jean being Jean. Although he did pester me about it quite a bit."

"He insisted he had been serious. That he even wanted to fire his lead at the last minute so you could have the part. He said, and I quote, 'Finn, can you imagine how radiant Ella would have been on the silver screen? I was obsessed by the image. Haunted. Possessed. But she refused.'"

"Jean may be a genius, but everyone fucks up from time to time. Not all his ideas are winners. I'm a philosopher, not a performer. I never gave it a single thought."

"I bet he was right. You would have been captivating. Mesmerizing. No doubt about it. You could have been a big star."

She giggled. "Lucky for me, I married one instead. Suits me better, don't you think?"

Finn laughed and gave her a kiss. He pulled back and said, "Jean hired Georgia because she looks just like you, sounds like you, moves like you. He told me, 'I always longed to see Ella on the big screen. Now instead I have your daughter.'"

"Best not to tell Georgia that!"

Finn laughed. "No shit. Jean did say she's perfect for the part."

"She'll do a fantastic job. I'm sure she and Jean will get along famously now that they have a chance to get to know each other better."

"Don't you find it curious? It's like for his last picture he's trying to capture something he wanted with you but couldn't have. I wonder what the film is really about."

Ella huffed. "He's always tackling the big topics. For his final film I can only imagine he's chasing something especially grand, something important to him. I guess we'll have to wait and see."

"I'm sure it will be something special. Georgia will grow a lot."

"I just hope . . ."

"What, love?" Finn asked.

"Yes, the kids are all doing amazing things this summer, but I hope they manage to have some fun too. Live a little. Live a lot. This glorious life goes by in a flash," Ella said.

"Speaking of living, with all this talk of the kids, we haven't given much thought to how *we're* going to spend this summer. Now that we've both slowed down a bit in our careers, we have time. My next film doesn't start shooting until late fall. You're in between books."

"What do you have in mind?" she asked.

"I know it's tradition for the honeymoon to follow the wedding, but this is a vow renewal and we never cared much about conventions anyway. Let's go on a spectacular trip this summer. We could go anywhere in the world. Hell, we could go around the whole world. Are you up for an adventure?"

Ella smiled. "Always."

"Where should we go?"

"Anywhere but Iceland. Georgia would have a fit."

They both laughed.

"Finn . . ."

"Yeah, sweetheart?"

"Thank you for turning my whole life into an adventure."

He kissed her tenderly. "Come on, let's go up to your office and give the old globe a spin. I'm hoping it lands on some little island where I can watch you running around on a white sand beach."

CHAPTER 4

Betty and Khalil were walking down the hospital corridor after rounds.

"How's Kate O'Connor doing?" Khalil asked.

"She's great," Betty replied with a smile.

"It's cute how she's your favorite patient."

"Doctors aren't supposed to have favorites," she replied matter-of-factly, before leaning closer and quietly confessing, "but between us, yeah, I really like her." Khalil smiled and Betty continued, "Kate's a modern-day superwoman. Instead of getting distracted chasing some Prince Charming fantasy, she focused on building a career. Now she's got a corner office on Wall Street and the guys follow her lead. As if that's not enough, she was like, 'I want to be a mother, so I'm doing it on my own.' Such a total badass." She stopped to giggle. "She's also wickedly funny. Dirtiest sense of humor. Has me laughing hysterically during every exam. Today it was a bit about how there should be more pregnant porn stars, for instructional purposes."

He laughed. "I still can't believe you came straight here from the airport."

"You know me, work is my life." He started to mutter a response when she continued, "Besides, you've been here for days without me. Can't let you race past me."

"Not a chance. You're the best one in the program," Khalil assured her as he opened the door to the residents' lounge.

She smiled bashfully, dropped on the couch, and announced, "I'm starving."

"I figured you would be. I ordered us food. From that new Indian place you wanted to try. It should be here any minute."

"Thank you. That was sweet," she replied.

Soon they were eating dinner and laughing uproariously. Betty was devouring the vindaloo. "This is awesome. Best curry I've had in ages."

Khalil tried to smile, but it came out as a strange, pained expression.

"Too hot?" she asked with a giggle as he gulped his water.

"Nah, it's all good," he gasped, his forehead glistening.

"Here, dip this in the raita. It will bring some relief," she said, handing him a piece of naan.

"Thanks," he said, and took a bite. "That's better."

She smiled.

"So, how was your weekend? Did you have a good time with your family?" he asked.

"Yeah, it was great. Too short. They asked about you. Said to send their regards."

"That was kind."

"It turns out I'll be going back again this fall. My parents celebrate their thirtieth anniversary on the first of October. They're renewing their vows," she said with a playful eye roll. "It's just so them. Hopeless romantics. Super weird."

"They have quite the iconic love story. I admit, I've seen pictures of their famous engagement at the Cannes Film Festival."

"Have you been googling me?" Betty joked.

Khalil laughed. "Maybe I'm just trying to figure out how someone who descends from a classic Hollywood fairy tale could be so anti-romance."

"Oh, please. I'm just a realist. If it makes you feel better, I was obsessed with fairy tales when I was little. I fancied myself a princess waiting to be swept away into a grand love story."

He seemed stunned by the admission. "So what happened?"

"I grew up, realized that 'happily ever after' is ridiculous, threw away the tiara, and picked up the schoolbooks."

"But your parents, they . . ."

"They're freaks of nature. Madly in love. I'll give you that."

"When I met your parents, they seemed completely down-to-earth. You'd never guess how famous they are. It's hard to imagine what it's like being the daughter of one of the biggest movie stars in the world. What was it like for you and your siblings growing up in the midst of Hollywood?"

"Our parents tried to keep things pretty normal for us. Once in a while we'd be out somewhere, and the paparazzi would hassle us. It freaked me out, so my dad would scoop me up to shield me until we could get away from them. Georgia, on the other hand, loved it. Even as a toddler she would laugh and make jokes, trying to get their attention. I think she thought they were following her!" Khalil laughed and she continued, "Seriously, my parents would have to drag her away! Albert's always been the shyest, the most private. It was the toughest on him. I could see it took a toll. He'd retreat into himself." She paused and added, "But like I said, it was only once in a while. Mostly, we lived like everyone else."

"You must have had fun going to movie premieres."

"Ha! Fat chance. I've never been to a single one."

"Seriously?" he asked with raised eyebrows.

"My dad sees acting as his work, not his life," Betty replied. "To him it's just about making cinematic art. And I told you, my parents tried to shield us from all the Hollywood stuff. They never took us to those kinds of events, even when Georgia was old enough to beg. They didn't want us exploited or scrutinized by the media. I think they were trying to let us figure out who we were in the most normal way possible. You know, if your version of normal includes a private jet," she said with a chuckle.

Khalil laughed. "Let me guess, you had a chauffeured limousine take you to school and a fleet of nannies to accommodate your every whim."

"I wish!" Betty replied with a laugh. She got quieter. "Seriously, though, my parents are awesome. We never had nannies or anything like that. They did everything themselves."

"Really? How did they juggle that with your father filming movies and your mother doing book tours and university fellowships? I just assumed that . . ."

She shook her head. "Honestly, I don't know how they managed it with three kids, but they did. We never had a nanny. My parents had a rule that we always stayed together as a family. So, we would all travel together when my dad had a location shoot or my mom had a fellowship. Whoever wasn't working would take care of us, but really, they both always did. They were super hands-on."

"That's amazing."

"Yeah. Even though we lived in a big house and flew on a jet, they tried to make things family-centered and DIY as much as they could." She laughed. "My mom was kind of extreme. When I was maybe six and Georgia was three, we wanted to make cookies in the shape of butterflies. Most parents would buy a cookie cutter. Not our mom. She taught us how to do it with what we already had at home. We made homemade sugar cookie dough. Then we used a butter knife to cut strips for the butterfly's body and a drinking glass to cut out circles, which we sliced in half. When faced opposite of each other, they looked like wings." Betty smiled. "The cookies really looked like butterflies. We each got to decorate half. I took so much time to make each one perfect. Georgia just dumped food coloring and colored sugar on hers Jackson Pollock style." Khalil laughed and she continued, "I realize now that my mom wanted us to be able to get by no matter what we had. To rely on our own creativity and imagination, not buying stuff or having it handed to us."

"What a wonderful gift," he remarked.

"Yeah, well, when I was a teenager, I would have loved it if they didn't make us set the table and do our own laundry and all that other kind of stuff that they could have easily outsourced, but in hindsight, I wouldn't change a thing. I know how lucky I am. In every way."

He smiled, unable to take his eyes off her. Softly, he whispered, "Betty . . ."

"So, should we clean this food up? You ready for a game of Scrabble? Medical terms only."

"Sure."

ALBERT GLANCED OVER AT RYAN AND their friends as their nearly empty trolley whizzed beneath the streets of Cambridge. Ryan bumped his shoulder and said, "Let's reenact our laser tag battle."

"Here?" Albert asked.

"Yeah," Ryan said, jumping up. "We have this car to ourselves."

Albert shook his head.

Ryan turned to their two friends. "Come on, guys."

The three began pretending they were in an adventure movie, using their hands as guns. Albert sat watching, a huge smile on his face.

"Come on, Al," Ryan encouraged, waving his hand. "Don't miss the moment."

Albert nodded and rose to join them. Soon it was a full-scale medieval battle, up and down the trolley car. After a series of clever moves that took out his opponents, Albert raised the toy sword he'd won at the arcade and declared, "I am king of laser tag, and you are my loyal subjects."

Ryan laughed. "See, aren't you glad I told you to pick the sword and not the stuffed animal?"

Albert had been smiling and laughing for so long, his face hurt. He thought about how many times in his life he had stood on the sidelines, too shy to join in, and how Ryan changed all that. He gazed at Ryan—his chiseled face with coffee-colored eyes and dark hair that effortlessly fell into place—and wondered how he could make everything so much fun, even a ride on the Red Line.

As the trolley turned the final corner, roaring into Harvard Station, Albert, Ryan, and their buddies grabbed onto each other to keep their balance. Albert and Ryan exchanged smiles as they all hopped off the train and headed back to their apartment building, joking and laughing along the short walk.

"Al and I are gonna hang for a while at his place," Ryan told his roommates, who headed into their apartment as Ryan followed Albert into his across the hall.

"That was so much fun," Ryan said as they both plopped onto the couch. "Don't get a big head, but it's true that you've become the king of laser tag. Glad you were my partner. We kicked their asses."

"I'd never go to places like that if it weren't, well, if it weren't for you. I'd probably spend all my time just drawing or reading. I lived in Boston for years before I even knew that arcade existed. I never played laser tag or any of that other stuff before I met you."

"I'm glad I bring you out of your shell," Ryan replied. Albert blushed and Ryan continued, "It's cute how into it you get. You come alive."

Albert smiled. "It's fun when we pretend to be characters, like we're in a TV show or action movie or something. It makes me feel . . ." He trailed off.

"What?" Ryan asked, taking his hand.

"I don't know. Like I'm not just me."

"There's nothing wrong with just being you," Ryan said, putting his hand on Albert's cheek. He kissed him softly and added, "I like you the way you are."

"I like you too," Albert replied, and they kissed again.

"So, since I dragged you out practically the second you got back, you never told me about your weekend at home."

"It was really nice just to spend time hanging out with my family. Sometimes it's hard being far away. I miss them. Georgia's hysterical. She always makes me laugh. You'd get a kick out of her. Betty's the smartest person I know. I like listening to her talk about her job. And my parents are great. They're into my new drawings and the classes I'm taking this summer."

"That's because you're super talented."

Albert blushed. "My folks celebrate their thirtieth anniversary on October first and they're doing a vow renewal, so we'll all be at that. My dad's flying us back home. So at least I know when I'll see them again."

"That's cool," Ryan said. "I actually have a couple relatives in LA. Maybe I can tag along with you, and we can have some fun in sunny Cali. There's an amazing arcade that has the sickest virtual reality stuff. Completely next level. We would have a blast."

Albert looked down and fidgeted.

Ryan touched his hand. "I wasn't asking you to introduce me to your family or anything. I just thought it would be a chance to go somewhere fun. It's not a big deal. Forget I mentioned it."

"Look, I know things were weird when I left. I thought about it. I thought about it a lot. The whole time I was gone."

"And?"

Albert looked into his eyes. "I want us to keep seeing each other, but I'm still not comfortable with public displays of affection."

"Al, all our friends know about us."

"I'm not worried about our friends. It's strangers. Friends of friends. Everyone takes pictures on their phones. When we're at an arcade or a party or someplace like that, I just need to lay off the physical stuff. The last thing I want is someone snapping a picture of us and posting it online for the whole world to see. My dad can't find out like that."

"What are the odds that's going to happen?"

"Being a celebrity's kid makes you a target," Albert explained. "It's hard to understand unless you've experienced it. I've dealt with it my whole life. I've been followed by the paparazzi. Kids at school have tried to become friends with me just to meet my parents. Sometimes I see people staring at me a little too long, pointing, whispering. All kinds of stuff. It makes me extremely uncomfortable."

"I'm sorry. That sucks. I guess I never really thought about what it's like. When we met, I didn't know who your parents were." Ryan ran his hand through his hair. "But . . ."

"What?" Albert asked.

"It's just that I guess some amount of that stuff is going to happen anyway. You can't let it stop you from living your life."

"I know, it's just that my dad doesn't know. I thought about telling him over the weekend. Honestly, I did. We were just all having such a good time, and I didn't want to mess it up."

"It's never going to be easy, but you'll feel so much better when you do it," Ryan replied. "From everything you've said about your dad, there's nothing to worry about. He sounds like a good guy."

"He's the best."

"So, how come you told your mother and not your father?"

"I didn't intend to." Albert took a moment and explained, "Junior year of high school I had a crush on this guy, Brett. I was too shy to do anything about it. I kind of watched him from a distance."

"Is he gay?" Ryan asked.

"Oh yeah. Totally open. He definitely dated and hooked up, but he never had a steady boyfriend or anything like that, so . . ." He took breath and continued, "It's stupid and embarrassing, but I always hoped that maybe he liked me back. He used to look at me sometimes. I thought that somehow we'd end up going out."

"What happened?"

Albert sighed. "One morning I was walking down the hallway in school, and he was coming toward me, holding hands with some other kid. People were whispering that they were going out. My heart sank. I was so distracted looking at them that I didn't notice there were a couple stairs in front of me. I flew down, falling flat on my stomach. All my stuff scattered everywhere. Some kids laughed, but Brett stopped to help me up." He got quiet for a moment before adding, "It was humiliating."

"That's horrible. I'm so sorry."

"Thanks. I forced myself to hold it together at school, but as soon as I got home, the floodgate burst. I exploded into tears and raced up to my room. My mother saw and followed me. She sat on my bed and threw her arms around me, rubbing my back, whispering that whatever it was would be okay." Ryan smiled softly and Albert continued, "When I finally calmed down, she asked me what happened. I just sat there, looking at her through puffy eyes, unable to speak. She took my hand, looked straight into my eyes, and said, 'Albert, I know exactly who you are. I do. And I love you with all my heart. You can tell me.' So, I told her everything."

"Wow. She sounds like an amazing mother."

"She's the sweetest person in the world."

"Are you sure she never told your father?"

Albert nodded. "She respects my privacy. She wanted me to tell him myself."

"Then . . ."

"I'm not ready yet. I'm working myself up to it. Can that just be okay? For a little while?"

Ryan leaned forward and kissed him. "We'll lay low on the public displays until you're ready."

Albert smiled and they kissed again.

GEORGIA RELAXED IN THE BACK SEAT, marveling at the unique landscape during the hour and a half drive from the Reykjavík airport. For all her travels, she had never seen any place like Iceland. At first there were seemingly endless vistas of moss-covered lava rocks with rolling milk chocolate–colored mountains in the distance. The stark terrain eventually gave way to vast green fields covered in mysterious purple flowers, punctuated with streams and waterfalls, and dotted with small horses that looked like they walked off the pages of a fable. Soon the landscape morphed again into a series of volcanoes and mountains, surrounded by rocks and dirt in all shades of brown. It was desolate and opulent all at once. She felt as if she had been dropped off on another planet.

"We're here," the driver announced as he pulled into the dirt driveway of a rustic-looking home facing a massive midnight-black volcano, no other signs of life as far as the eye could see.

They spilled out of the vehicle, and the driver began unloading her luggage from the trunk. Georgia took a deep breath and looked at the volcano. He noticed and said, "Don't worry, she won't blow. You're a safe distance. There's a trail if you're adventurous. It's quite beautiful."

She smiled and followed him into the house. An older couple with snow-colored hair hurried over to greet her, warm smiles on their faces. "Welcome. I am Ástríður and this is my husband Gunnar."

"Hi. I'm Georgia Sinclair Forrester."

"Yes, of course," Ástríður said. "My husband and I are the caretakers. This property is usually used as an artists' residency house. We host visitors from all over. Mr. Mercier rented it during the duration of your film shoot. The cabin that's being used as the set is just down the road. There are trailers set up for the actors, and a car will take you back and forth." Georgia nodded and she continued, "So, about the house. Common rooms are on this floor: a living room with a television and an old DVD collection, a kitchen that you're free to use, a dining room where meals are served, and there's also a self-serve bar and a large workspace that can be used as an office, a rehearsal room, or some have even used it to do yoga, as there's a sublime view. There's also a small library and an even smaller gym. Just a treadmill, an elliptical machine, and some free weights. Guest rooms are on the second floor. You'll be in seven at the end of the hallway," she said, holding out an old-fashioned skeleton key.

"Thank you," Georgia replied.

"Mr. Mercier and Mr. Hennesey are relaxing in the dining room. I can take you to join them if you like. I've put out afternoon refreshments. Dinner will be served in a couple hours. My husband can assist the driver with your bags. Unless you prefer to get settled in your room."

"No, I'd love to join the others, please."

"Right this way," Ástríður said, while the men ferried the luggage upstairs.

Georgia followed her into a casual dining room featuring wood furniture that matched the floors, with a wall of windows overlooking the volcano. Jean and Michael were sitting at the oval-shaped table, with pots of coffee and tea and a smattering of bite-size sandwiches, pastries, and fruit.

"Georgia!" Michael bellowed, jumping up to hug her. "Great to see you."

"You too," she replied.

Jean slowly rose, leaning on his chair for support as he labored to his feet. He looked at her with a glint in his eyes and in his thick French accent said, "*Ma chérie*, welcome," before pecking her on each cheek.

Michael lent Jean a hand as they all sat down.

"Wow, that view is something. I've never seen any place like this," Georgia remarked.

"It's wild, isn't it?" Michael asked. "We're definitely not in Hollywood anymore."

Georgia giggled. "It should be an amazing backdrop for filming. So otherworldly."

Jean smirked. "The landscape is actually ugly in a way, all the brown and black rocks and dirt as far as one can see. Yet it's spectacularly beautiful and singular too. Breathtaking. Almost as if the ugliness has turned inward on itself, creating something extraordinary, something one can hardly turn away from." He stopped to huff before adding, "Beauty from despair. Like much in this fucked-up wasteland we call life."

"Glad to see age hasn't softened those hard edges," Michael joked. He and Georgia both laughed.

Jean shrugged. "We are who we are. Life is what it is."

"And on that dystopian note, tea or coffee?" Michael asked Georgia, gesturing at the pots.

"Perhaps something a little stiffer after the journey. There's a bar over there," Jean said, pointing to the corner. "Your mother has always enjoyed a good bourbon. Your father as well."

"Maybe tonight after dinner. For now, tea would be lovely."

"How are your folks?" Michael asked as he poured the tea.

"They're great. Same as always. You know how they are. It's like they're starring in an epic love story. They can't get enough of each other, even after decades together. Betty and I think it's super weird," she replied, making a face. "When I landed, I got a text letting us know they're going on some grand trip around the world this summer. Oh, and their thirtieth wedding anniversary is coming up, so they're doing a vow renewal." Georgia rolled her eyes. "Hopeless romantics."

The subtlest smile flickered across Jean's wrinkled face. "Michael, do you remember when Ella and Finn met, during our summer together in Sweden?"

"Oh, yeah," Michael replied. He looked at Georgia and said, "Your father fell for your mother the second he laid eyes on her. She was a knockout. There was a spark between them. A palpable connection right from the start. We all saw it."

"They're pretty much a fairy tale. It's so strange," Georgia said. "I mean, who in the real world gets hit by lightning the moment they meet someone and then rides off into the sunset? Who even believes in that?"

Jean's eyes were intense. He looked as if he was studying her. "You remind me so much of your mother when she was younger, not just your beauty. Ella was always a free spirit too . . . bohemian ideals, wanderlust. She wasn't exactly ready for your father."

Georgia raised her eyebrows quizzically and opened her mouth, but before she could say anything, Michael said, "Yeah, well we were all young then. Hell, I slept with half the crew and extras on that set. That was before Lauren and I got serious, of course."

"You don't have to explain it to me," Georgia said. "I can't imagine being tied down. There's a lot to be said for casual lovers, going with the flow, living freely."

"Jean's right. You're so much like your mother. That must scare the hell out of your father!" Michael joked.

Georgia giggled. "What can I say? I'm all for great sex and big adventures, just not fairy tales."

Jean pursed his lips, a twinkle in his eyes. He opened his mouth, but Ástríður walked into the room with a tall, dark-haired young man in tow. "Mr. Reed is here," she announced, before scurrying away.

"Jean, it's wonderful to see you," Rupert said in his British accent. "You as well, Michael. My mother asked me to send her regards to you both," he added, shaking their hands. He turned to Georgia and fell silent, staring at her as if no one else were there, his mouth slightly agape. After a moment, he caught himself and stuttered, "Uh, hello, I'm Rupert. My uh, my friends call me Roo." She rose to shake his hand, noticing his striking blue eyes and rosy cheeks. "Forgive my cold hands. They don't call it Iceland for nothing, I suppose," he finished with a warm smile.

"It's a pleasure. I'm Georgia."

He gazed deeply into her eyes like he couldn't turn away. "Uh, forgive me. Travel day. Made the mistake of renting a car and driving myself from the airport, so it's been harrowing." She smiled and he continued, "I've seen some of your work, but you're even more beautiful in person. How is it possible?"

She looked down, blushing, and then looked into his eyes and said, "Thank you."

A long moment passed, their gazes locked and no words spoken, as if they were suspended in time.

Jean and Michael exchanged a glance. Eventually, Michael cleared his throat and said, "Roo, how about some hot tea to warm up?"

"Ah, yes, sure," Roo stammered, his eyes still glued to Georgia. They smiled bashfully at one another and sat down.

Jean looked them over, smirked, and muttered, "Just like Ella, indeed."

CHAPTER 5

The next morning, Georgia headed down to the gym for an early workout and saw Roo jogging on the treadmill. "Oh, hello," she said.

He hit pause, caught his breath as the machine slowed, and smiled. "Good morning. Did you sleep well?"

She nodded. "And you?"

"Passed out. Travel days always do that." He wiped his brow and said, "Listen, I apologize if yesterday I was a bit, um, well, out of sorts. I didn't mean to gawk or make you uncomfortable."

Georgia looked down.

"Like I'm probably doing again right now," he said with a sigh. "Sorry. I'm not usually such a bumbling fool. Suppose I haven't quite gotten my bearings yet."

"You're not making me uncomfortable," she assured him.

For a moment they just looked at each other, their gazes connected, until Roo stammered, "Uh, you came for a workout? Well, obviously. Did you want the treadmill?"

"Oh, I don't want to interrupt . . ."

"Nonsense," he insisted, stepping down. "I'll jump on the elliptical."

"Thank you," she replied. "Ástríður wasn't kidding when she said the gym was small. It's a shoebox."

"Indeed. But perhaps there's something to be said about only having what you really need. Getting back to the basics."

"Yeah. It's sort of charming," Georgia agreed.

"Well, I'll stop blabbering on so you can get to it."

She smiled, pressed the start button, and began running.

Nearly forty-five minutes later, Georgia hit stop, grabbed a small towel, and wiped her sweaty brow.

Roo hit stop on the elliptical, saying, "Truth be told, I could have stopped twenty minutes ago, but I felt like I had better keep up with you, for fear of appearing like a wimp."

She giggled and tossed him a towel. "You know what it's like being on set all day. Never any time to move around, so I like to get a good workout in the mornings. Keeps my energy up."

"Water?" he asked, filling a cup from the pitcher.

"Please," she replied, taking the cup.

They both guzzled their water.

"Well, I should go shower," Georgia said.

"I best do the same. Meet you at breakfast?"

She nodded.

GEORGIA BOUNDED INTO THE DINING ROOM to see Roo sitting alone and sipping his tea at the only table in the room.

"Saved you a seat," he said with a goofy smile.

She giggled and sat opposite him.

"I didn't know if you prefer tea or coffee," he said, gesturing at the two pots on the table. "Or perhaps something else altogether. Tomato juice? Kombucha? Canned energy drink? Ginger beer?"

"Ginger beer? Does anyone drink that for breakfast?"

"No, probably not. But you strike me as someone who marches to your own beat. Thought it was worth a stab."

She smiled. "Tea. I drink black tea in the mornings."

"Ah, surprising for an American," he said as he poured her a cup.

"My mother's a tea drinker. I probably got it from her. Plus, we traveled a lot when I was growing up. Spent a fair amount of time in England, China, all over. I guess I got used to some of the customs."

"Right, you must have traveled for—" Roo was interrupted when Ástríður came into the room.

"Good morning. What can I get you two for breakfast today? Eggs? Oatmeal? Yogurt? Fruit?" she asked.

"Oh, should we wait for the others?" Georgia asked.

"Mr. Mercier is already on set. He left quite early."

"My mum told me Michael is always the last one down to breakfast, racing to make his call time," Roo added. "We best not wait. Please, after you."

"Yogurt with some berries or other fruit, please," Georgia said.

"Two eggs over easy, with toast, please. Jam if you have it," Roo said.

"Certainly. Don't worry, if Mr. Hennesey joins you, we'll fix him something straight away," Ástríður replied before scurrying off.

"So, you were saying you traveled a lot growing up. For your parents' work?" Roo asked.

"Yes. They always wanted to keep us together, so we'd jet off to wherever either of them was working, for my mom's university fellowships or my dad's movies. I loved it. Especially the location shoots for my dad's films. It was exciting creating a new home in places that felt exotic, and knowing we were there because my dad was a star making a movie. That seemed so special." She stopped, crinkled her nose, and shook her head. "To me, it was like a dream. In some ways it set the tone for how I aspire to live."

Roo smiled, captivated by her every word.

"And you?" she asked. "Did you travel much for your parents' work?"

"Not really. My father is English to the core. Has more than a bit of a bias toward London theater. Thinks it's the best in the world, you know, more serious or some such thing. He always staged his plays around town. My mum traveled a bit for films, but most of her career was on London's stages or in indie films shot around England, at least after I was born. She did shoot a picture in Ireland one summer and we all went, lived in a cottage. It was quite lovely. The Irish countryside is gorgeous if you don't mind the rain, which as a Londoner I was used to."

"Do you still live in London?"

"I do. I rent a flat in an old brownstone. Beautiful original wood floors and crown moldings, on a tree-lined street. I'm happy there, although I love to travel. I'm not wedded to London like my parents. I could see myself making a home just about anywhere."

Georgia smiled.

"And you? Do you live in California?"

"I sort of hop around from place to place, for work. Do short-term apartment rentals where I'm never there long enough to fully unpack my things. When an exciting project comes my way, I love having the freedom to pick up, immerse myself, live somewhere new. When I'm in between projects, I usually go back to LA, or I take a long vacation and veg on the beach until the next job."

"I understand that adventurous, backpacking spirit. Sometimes I think we actors chose this line of work because we're road dogs by nature."

"Yeah, I've always thought of it like running away to join the circus," Georgia joked.

"I've spent a fair amount of time in LA myself. These days it's a must in our industry. I'm not terribly enamored by the Hollywood thing, but the landscape in Southern California is spectacular. For one job the studio rented me a little flat in the canyons. There are the most incredible hiking trails."

"It's one of the great things about LA," she said. "Lots of places to run and hike. I love getting a good workout without having to be stuck inside. It's how I clear my mind. I think it's a dopamine rush or something. The endorphins combined with the vitamin D."

"Perhaps one morning we can take a hike around the volcano," Roo suggested. "It's not exactly the temperate climate you're used to, but it certainly looks too unique to pass up."

"That would be great. I'm always up for an adventure."

He smiled. "Me too."

Just then, Ástríður came into the room and served their breakfast.

"Thank you," Georgia said.

"Yes, thank you. Looks great," Roo added.

"My pleasure. Please let me know if I can get you anything else," she said before leaving them to their meal.

"Well, bon appétit," Georgia said.

"Bon appétit."

Georgia picked up her spoon, but Roo just sat, staring at her. She noticed and gazed at him. A long moment passed before he said, "At the risk of needing to apologize again, I must tell you that you have the most extraordinary green eyes."

She smiled and softly said, "Thank you."

Their eyes were glued to one another as if neither could look away.

"Georgia," Roo muttered.

Just then, Michael came vaulting into the room. "Hey, guys. What did I miss?"

THE THREE ACTORS WERE SHUTTLED TO the set, a pristine log cabin surrounded by rolling green mountains with an ethereal quality. As they spilled out of the vehicle, Georgia muttered, "Wow. It looks like someplace mythical creatures would live or something."

"It's extraordinary," Roo agreed.

"If not for the trailers and crew scattered everywhere, you'd never guess a movie was going to be made here. There's something untouched about it," Michael remarked.

Jean's assistant ran to greet them. He escorted them each to their personal trailers to drop off their belongings and meet with wardrobe before heading to the hair and makeup trailer. Soon the actors were called to set. As they ambled over, Michael said, "Guys, just a heads-up that Jean's unconventional to say the least. Don't be surprised if you don't have a clue what's going on. The last time I did a film with him, we had no idea what was going on for weeks, except that he seemed pissed off. The first day was a blur."

"I'm up for anything," Georgia said.

"Me too. Looking forward to it," Rupert added.

When they arrived on set, the crew was milling about. Jean hollered, "Everyone, listen up!" and the room fell silent. "I'd like to introduce our stars. Michael Hennesey is playing a reclusive Pulitzer Prize–winning author dying of cancer."

Michael trotted to the center of the room to applause.

"Rupert Reed as his biographer, hired to write his memoir," Jean said.

Roo stepped beside Michael to more cheers.

"Georgia Sinclair Forrester as the young woman he hired to help with domestic tasks—and the love interest of both men."

Georgia joined her castmates to more applause.

Jean addressed the actors directly. "Today we are shooting the scene where Rupert's and Georgia's characters meet. He has been sent off doing research for the past week, and while he's been gone, she was hired. There is nothing simple about this scene as it foreshadows how both men come to feel about her and the complex relations between all three. With minimal dialogue, it will all be in your eyes."

The actors exchanged supportive looks.

"Places, everyone," Jean commanded.

The actors scurried to hit their marks, although with a sparse script and no blocking or rehearsals, they all seemed a bit unsure of themselves. Georgia was at the kitchen counter fidgeting with a prop, Michael seated at the table, his leg jiggling, and Roo outside the door slowly rocking back and forth. The actors immediately snapped into their characters when Jean called, "Rolling . . . Action!"

Georgia picked up a quiche and said, "It's cool now." As she turned toward the table, Roo knocked on the door and then stepped inside. The two immediately caught each other's eyes and stopped in their tracks, as if frozen.

Eventually he stammered, "Uh, sorry to interrupt. I didn't know you had company."

She smiled shyly and then placed the quiche on the table. Michael noticed how they looked at each other and grumbled, "This is the American girl I hired to help out around here, Giselle. She may also be of some assistance to you sorting through those boxes of my old papers. Join me for lunch."

"It's lovely to meet you," the young biographer said as he sat down.

"It's nice to meet you too," she replied. She retrieved an extra plate and set of cutleries, placed them on the table, and asked, "Would you like coffee?"

"Please."

She filled a mug and set it in front of him.

"Thank you," he replied softly, their eyes lingering on one another.

"I've heard all about your book project," she said. "I just hope you don't work too hard. Someone here needs his rest too."

A trace of a smile flickered across Michael's face, and he patted her hand. "See, she's taking very good care of me."

"Well, if you two gentlemen don't need anything else, I'm going to take a drive to the pharmacy to pick up those prescriptions. I'll stop at the market on the way back. Is there anything special you'd like?" she asked her employer.

"Only your return."

She smiled and headed to the door.

"Giselle," Roo called.

She turned toward him.

"Thank you for lunch. A real pleasure to meet you."

"See you later," she replied.

The men watched as she exited and then looked at each other as if they were both afraid to be the first to exhale.

"Cut!" Jean hollered.

The crew began milling around as the actors all huddled together for notes.

"I'm at a loss. I've never had a first shot like that," Jean said, shaking his head.

"That bad?" Michael asked with raised eyebrows.

"It was completely natural. None of that damn acting I detest. The way you two looked at each other," he said to Roo and Georgia, "it was perfect."

The actors all beamed, surprised by the praise.

"Let's do it again. Try not to fuck it up," Jean said. "Places, everyone . . . Rolling . . . Action!"

AFTER A LONG DAY ON SET, JEAN INSTRUCTED the actors to change into their street clothes and meet in the dining room for dinner, which was to be their nightly routine. Michael elected himself bartender and fixed himself a vodka tonic and bourbon neat for the others. "You seemed uncharacteristically pleased today," Michael said to Jean as he passed out the cocktails.

"Actors so often disappoint. They fail miserably when they try to act. They must live it, breathe it, surrender to it. You can't find truth when you're busy pretending." He paused, glanced at Georgia and Roo, and said, "Some things cannot be forced. They must be genuine. Then there is the chance for something beautiful." Jean raised his glass. "A toast. To the least abysmal first day on set I recall." The actors raised their glasses and began to smile when he added, "But don't let it go to your heads. We shall see what happens tomorrow."

Michael laughed. They all clinked glasses and took a sip.

"That's smooth," Roo said.

"I like the vanilla undertones," Georgia remarked.

Ástríður and Gunnar came in and presented dinner family style: roasted local fish, braised lamb stew, potatoes, and vegetables. Michael assisted Jean and the others helped themselves. As they began eating, Michael said, "So, Jean, since this is your last film, any plans for your retirement?"

Jean huffed. "I think only about what I am doing now. The film is all-consuming. She is everything."

"You gonna tell us what it's really about? There's always so much meaning embedded in your projects that's hard to see until it all comes together," Michael said.

"Don't worry about it," Jean replied.

Michael chuckled. "Here I thought maybe age had relaxed you. I can see you haven't changed a bit."

"Damn right," Jean agreed.

"Well, I for one am enjoying the process," Roo said.

"Me too. I never like to overthink things," Georgia said.

Jean smirked. "Good, then you shall be open to the moments." He skimmed his finger around the rim of his glass. "That's all there is, really. Moments. In life. In film. You string them together and somehow they become a story."

"Sounds like you're getting a little sentimental there," Michael remarked.

"Eh, rubbish," Jean protested, downing the rest of his drink. "But I'll tell you this, as the one nearest the grave at the table, best to focus on the moments. Live them, create them, bloody well steal them if you must. That's where beauty hides. There is so much ugliness in this fucked-up abyss of human tragedy. Even beauty is bound to and corrupted by its underside. But on those rarest of occasions, glimmers of pure beauty can be found. It always hides in the moments."

They all sat quietly soaking in the words, until Jean broke the silence. "Such a serious lot. Will be a damn long summer if you don't lighten up. Michael, another bourbon. Then perhaps you'll all indulge me with your stories of being overly pampered actors. Booze. Bravado. Broken chandeliers in hotel rooms. Don't hold back."

AFTER DINNER, MICHAEL AND JEAN RETIRED for the evening. Roo turned to Georgia and said, "It's still a bit early. I was thinking about another drink and perhaps checking out that DVD collection Ástríður mentioned. Care to join me?"

"I'd love to," she replied.

Roo topped off their drinks and they strolled to the dimly lit living room.

"Wow, this is so old-school," Georgia said, noticing the movie collection as she plopped onto the couch.

"Their selection is too. Seems they have a fondness for the classics. What type of film do you feel like?"

"Anything. Your choice."

"Oh my. They have *Monty Python and the Holy Grail*. Have you seen it?"

She shook her head.

"It's one of my favorites. Sort of an English tradition. It's a comedy. Satirical and arguably quite stupid. It was banned by all kinds of religious groups."

"You sold me," she said with a giggle.

"I knew you were a rebel." He put the DVD in the machine and hit play, taking the seat beside her. "It really is a very particular kind of humor. If you find it dreadful, say the word and we'll put something else on. I won't be offended."

"I'm up for anything," she assured him.

Within moments they were both laughing uproariously. They spent the next hour and a half laughing so hard Georgia complained, "My stomach actually hurts."

"So, you liked it?" he asked.

"Adored it. Although I don't know why. Somehow it walked a fine line between totally stupid and epically brilliant."

"Yes, exactly," Roo agreed.

They found themselves staring at one another, silly smiles on their faces.

Eventually Georgia said, "I can't believe how well things went today. It felt like we all just clicked into our characters."

"Yeah. Jean seemed quite pleased. Listening to him at dinner tonight . . ."

"What?" she asked.

"I'm not sure, really. It's just he has such a reputation for being hopelessly dark and dystopian, and while on the surface that rings true, there's a real depth and sensitivity there that surprise me."

"I feel that way too," she agreed. "I'm looking forward to getting back on set. Taking it day by day. Well, moment by moment."

They smiled at one another, and Roo said, "Speaking of the film, we should probably get some rest. I fear I've kept you up too late already."

"No, this was great. But you're right. We should probably get a good night's sleep before tomorrow."

"I'll walk you up," he offered.

When they arrived at Georgia's room, she said, "This is me. Thanks for a fun night. I'll have to see the rest of those movies."

"Glad you're a fan. Well, good night." He turned to leave and then swiveled around and said, "See you in the gym in the morning?"

"Yeah. See you there. Good night."

Roo began puttering down the hallway but turned just as she unlocked her door. She glanced over and they smiled at each other before she disappeared into her room.

# CHAPTER 6

The next morning, Roo ambled into the dining room to see that Georgia was already there, scribbling in a notebook. He watched her for a moment before saying, "You beat me."

She looked up and smiled. "I did get a jump start since you were still lifting weights after my run."

"Ah, yes," he said, taking the seat opposite her. "I also confess to indulging in a long, hot shower. Something had me a bit giddy this morning, and I found myself humming in the shower."

"I didn't know you Englishmen got giddy, stiff upper lip and all."

"Perhaps my new American friend has brought it out of me," he replied with a smile. He paused before adding, "I like starting the day with you, spending time with you. Well, I just like you."

"I like you too," she said. They were silent for a moment before Georgia gestured to the pot in the center of the table, "Uh, there's plenty of tea."

"Thank you," he said, topping hers off and then pouring himself a cup. "Have I disturbed you?" he asked, glancing at her notebook.

"Not at all," she assured him, pushing it aside. "I've been journaling since I was a kid. I try to write every day, but time got away from me yesterday."

"That's a wonderful habit. Do you use it for reflection or to document your life?"

"Both, really. When I was a kid, I had such big dreams. I'd write them down. Guess I thought it made them more real. As I got older, it became more of a way to chronicle my life. The theater productions I've done, films, travel. I'm the kind of person who always wants to live in the moment, but I guess . . ." She trailed off.

"What?" Roo asked, gazing at her with his warm eyes.

"I want to remember too."

They were smiling at each other when Ástríður came to take their breakfast order.

"Good morning. What can I get you both?" she asked.

"Good morning. Yogurt and berries again, please," Georgia replied.

"Two eggs, toast, and jam, please," Roo said.

After she left, Roo said, "For two adventure seekers, we are also creatures of habit, I suppose. Anyway, you were saying that you like to capture your experiences. Do you ever intend to do anything with your journals, such as writing a memoir?"

"Oh, I don't think so. What about you? Do you write at all?"

"Well, yes. I don't think I've dared to say it aloud before, but I write scripts. Plays, films. I have several drafted, and bits of many more. Something to keep me busy in my trailer and on days off."

"That's so cool," Georgia said. "Why keep that to yourself?"

"Well, it's a little tough walking the same path as my parents. As an actor, I'm constantly compared to my mother. I always understood that would be the case, and I have no hard feelings. I realize my name has opened more doors than it's closed. But that sort of scrutiny can be a lot. My writing feels so personal to me. I think perhaps it's my true calling. My father's such a successful playwright. To go down that road of comparison again, well, I'm just not ready for it. I'm sure you know how it is."

"I do," she said compassionately. "Everyone looks at me as Finn Forrester's daughter. He's the greatest dad in the world and I admire him so much as an actor, but I want to make my own mark too, be my own person, create my own body of work, my own artistic legacy. I try to focus on the positives, though. I've learned so much about storytelling and the business from him." She brushed a stray curl away from her eyes and quietly said, "Roo . . ."

"Yes?"

"I hope you don't mind me saying this, but don't let other people stop you from being yourself. Write your scripts. When you're ready, try to get them produced. Make your mark as a playwright if that's what you love. Besides, it's smart for actors to create projects for themselves. It will help you captain your own ship, however you choose."

"I think that's just what I needed to hear. Thank you." She smiled and he continued, "Do you ever write any material for yourself, you know, an acting role?"

"No. But I do write . . ." Georgia stopped herself and looked down.

"Please, tell me."

"Songs," she said, looking into his eyes. "I write songs about stuff I'm going through."

"That's wonderful."

"I bring an acoustic guitar with me everywhere. It's in my room. I'm not very good, but I can play enough to accompany myself."

"Do you ever want to . . ."

"No," she said, shaking her head. "It's just a personal creative outlet, like my journals, but artistic. I'm definitely an actress. No plans to become an actor-turned-singer. It's something that's just for me."

"How special to have that for yourself."

"Thanks. Most people have the impression that I don't want to do anything that doesn't get me some kind of attention. I mean, I've never shied away from public life. Pursued acting relentlessly. The spotlight. Couldn't wait to walk my first red carpet. But I have a private side too, and I think it's good to keep that."

"You know, I was really looking forward to working with you," he said.

"You were?"

Roo nodded. "You're far more spectacular than I could have imagined. Full of surprises in the most extraordinary way."

Georgia looked down, blushing. "You're surprising too, in the most extraordinary way."

"That may be the best compliment I've ever received, coming from you."

She leaned forward and put her hand on the table. He reached out, but before they made contact, Ástríður came in to deliver their food and they slunk back into their seats.

"ARE YOU UP FOR ANOTHER MOVIE NIGHT?" Roo asked Georgia after dinner.

"Absolutely," she replied, and they moseyed to the living room.

"You pick this time," he said.

"How about we take turns?"

"Deal. So, what are we in for tonight?" he asked, taking a seat on the couch.

Georgia scanned the selection. "Ooh, they have *Breakfast at Tiffany's*. It's my favorite."

"Then let's watch."

"How about we save it?" She continued surveying the selection. "Seems they have a bunch of Audrey Hepburn's films. There's *Roman Holiday*, which could be a nice escape. But if you prefer something else . . ."

"I'd love to watch it with you. I have a fondness for the classics, and anything with a good setting."

Georgia smiled, put on the DVD, and curled up on the couch.

They sat quietly enjoying the movie, giggling and glancing at each other at the exact same moments. When it ended, Georgia said, "Thanks for indulging me."

"My pleasure. That was fun. Makes me want to visit Rome again."

"Oh, me too. They must have had an amazing time filming that."

"Indeed. Benefit of being an actor," he replied. "Location shoots are few and far between these days, but there's nothing like it for the cast, and you can see and feel the difference in the films."

"I think so too."

"I know you're a road dog by nature, but perhaps location shoots are even more special to you because of your family history. I mean, you descend from one of the most famous, talked-about film shoots of all time. My mother says that while on-set love affairs have a reputation for fizzling quickly, she knew your parents would last a lifetime."

Georgia smiled. "They're a total fairy tale. It's kind of crazy. I guess they were perfect from the start. It's . . ." She stopped and looked down.

"What?" he asked sweetly.

She looked into his eyes and said, "It's kind of intense, thinking about how their love story is intertwined with film history and with this real-life movie moment on a red carpet in front of the world. It's hard to explain, but it's kind of like living in a myth or something, but it's real, as impossible as that may seem."

Roo smiled. "Yes, I can imagine it's a mind trip, perhaps more so for you as an actress yourself."

"Yeah. Of course, my parents' story isn't the typical Hollywood tale. After all, my mother isn't in the business. It was just chance that she was there when they were filming, thanks to her friendship with Jean."

"Remarkable how much in life happens by chance. Or perhaps it's fate."

They sat for a moment, comfortably looking at each other before Georgia said, "So, we'll be doing one of our big scenes tomorrow. Are you nervous?"

He shook his head. "We'll get through it together. I'm looking forward to it."

"Me too." Another moment passed, their gazes locked before she added, "Well, we should probably get some rest."

"Indeed. I'll walk you up."

"Roo, this morning when you said you like spending time with me . . ."

"Yes?"

"I just want you to know how much I like spending time with you too."

Roo smiled. "Thank you for both a wonderful start and a wonderful end to my day. Come on, let's get some sleep."

"LISTEN UP!" JEAN CALLED, AND EVERYONE settled down. "This is an extremely intimate scene. There's the growing, palpable desire between Rupert's and Georgia's characters, but also the revealing nature of the documents they are sorting, and then the look on his face when Michael's character eavesdrops. Without any touching, it will all be in your expressions and tone of voice. Be delicate. Places, everyone."

The actors scampered to their marks. Georgia and Roo were seated on the floor with stacks of papers in front of them and several cardboard boxes scattered about. Michael was out of the camera's eye, waiting to walk to the door.

"Rolling . . . Action!"

Roo and Georgia began sorting through documents, and with the piles around them, it looked as though they had been at it for some time.

"When he hired me to write his memoir, I didn't quite know what I was in for."

"Yeah, it's hard to believe how many notes and clippings he kept," she said.

"Well, sure, but I was referring to his . . ."

"What?" she asked, pausing to look at him.

"He's a bit gruff and demanding. Always seems angry, or at least unhappy. Perhaps except for when you're around. You have such a gentle way. It seems to transform him from a lion to a puppy. He's softer when you're here." The corners of her mouth curled upward ever so slightly, and he added, "I can hardly blame him. It seems impossible not to be in better spirits near you."

Her smile grew modestly as their gazes held each other. After a moment passed, she returned her attention to the papers. "I'm glad to bring him some comfort, take care of him. It's hard to imagine how difficult it is, well . . ."

"Preparing to die?" he said.

She nodded. "I find it a bit strange he left his home, came here to the middle of nowhere, and now we're the only two people in his life. Seems like a time when most would want to be with their loved ones. It's so beautiful here, but it's like he slunk off to die all alone." She stopped and shook her head. "I guess it just makes me a bit sad for him."

"In the literary world, he has a reputation for being a notorious reclusive. If it helps, I think this is very much in line with how he has lived."

"I've never read his work. Do you admire him?" she asked.

"Immensely. He's an extraordinary writer. Brave. Unapologetic. He really pushed the envelope with narrative structure, not to mention the subjects he's written about. He's certainly not afraid of tragedy and suffering." He moved a pile of papers over and continued, "Of course, despite his enormous success, he's always had detractors. Critics have been bitterly divided. When he won the Pulitzer, there were protests. Sometimes he courted the uproar, wearing the controversial label like a badge of honor, and other times he may have been a bit baffled or offended by it. I think it's exacerbated his volatile side and explains why he's chosen to be so isolated."

Just then, Michael came to the doorway. Instead of stepping into the room, he stopped to listen.

"Why do you suppose he keeps all these negative reviews? Seems like something one would discard. There are piles of them, but none of the good ones nor any clippings about all the honors he's received," she remarked.

"I can't say for certain. Perhaps he's motivated by the criticisms. Or maybe it's a marker to him of how wrong they've been, those who failed to recognize his genius. Or maybe he sees them with humor."

"Or maybe part of him believes the bad stuff," she suggested.

Michael squeezed his eyelids shut for a moment.

"If I was a betting man, I'd wager he's not someone who wants to bask in the light. Perhaps some people are just more comfortable in the darkness."

"Well, I hope I can help bring him into the light. For whatever time he has left," she replied.

A soft smile crossed Michael's face.

"Giselle . . ." Roo whispered.

"Yes," she said, looking up into his eyes.

"I've never met anyone more filled with light and kindness than you. You're extraordinary and he's very lucky to have you. We both are." They sat, their gazes locked, their bodies only centimeters apart. Eventually he stammered, "Uh, we should probably get back to it. Thank you for helping me."

"It's my pleasure," she replied sweetly.

"Cut!" Jean hollered.

There was an immediate cacophony of noise from the crew. The actors convened to get notes.

"It's a bloody miracle because that was damn perfect. I don't want to lose our rhythm. Let's do it again so we can capture it from different angles. Places," Jean said.

Roo squeezed Georgia's hand and whispered, "You were brilliant."

"You were too. You made it easy," she whispered in return.

"No talking!" Jean commanded.

Georgia and Roo exchanged a mischievous giggle and resumed their positions.

"Rolling . . . Action!"

CHAPTER 7

A few days later as they waited for dinner, Jean raised his bourbon and said, "I'd like to make a toast. We are now six days into filming, and you have not disappointed me yet. I'm sure you'll fuck up eventually, so best to enjoy the moment."

The actors laughed, raised their glasses, and sipped their cocktails.

"Georgia, have you heard from your folks? Are they on their grand trip?" Michael asked.

"We got a text from them yesterday that they're in Australia, snorkeling at the Great Barrier Reef. Apparently, they're planning to work their way back, with stops in Asia and Europe, but they're keeping the itinerary secret. Knowing them, they're probably just sticking their finger on a map and seeing where they wind up."

Roo chuckled. "They sound like great adventure seekers."

"Yeah, it's pretty cool," Georgia conceded.

"You two have the next couple days off while Jean works me to the bone," Michael joked. "Any adventures of your own planned?"

Georgia glanced at Roo and shrugged. "I'm not sure really."

"Perhaps I'll convince her to take a hike around the volcano tomorrow morning. We've been talking about it all week," Roo said.

"It won't take much convincing. I'm in," Georgia said.

"Enjoy your time off. Next week we're shooting your big love scene, and I won't be going easy on you," Jean warned them.

Georgia and Roo glanced shyly at each other. Just then, their hosts came to serve dinner.

"SO, IT'S YOUR TURN TO PICK TONIGHT," Roo said, taking his usual seat on the couch.

"If you're still up for it, how about *Breakfast at Tiffany's?*" she asked.

"I'd love to watch with you."

She put the DVD on and got comfortable on the couch.

As they watched the film, Roo found himself looking at Georgia out of the corner of his eye: the glow of the screen on her face, her soft smile, and her eyes as if they were about to overflow. When the film ended, tears trickled down her cheeks. She turned to Roo, sniffled, and said, "I'm so embarrassed. I always cry at the end. I'm sorry."

"Never apologize for feeling. It's beautiful. Enchanting. I'm sure that emotional honesty is part of what makes you such an extraordinary actress."

She smiled through her tears and wiped her face. "As you've probably guessed, Audrey Hepburn is my all-time favorite. So uniquely beautiful, and there's such a vulnerability to her performances. Any actress would be lucky to have a small flicker of what she possessed."

"Funny, when we were filming this week, I thought you had all those qualities in droves," Roo said. "Obviously, you're stunning, but it's much more than that. There's such an honesty and depth to your performance; it's subtle, layered, and completely your own. It's mind-blowing to watch. I spent most of the week just hoping not to screw things up."

"I don't know what to say. That's so sweet."

"There's nothing that Hepburn or any other actress has on you."

Georgia blushed. "All the same could be said to you. There's such grace and ease in the way you work. I'm learning a lot from acting with you."

"Thank you," he said softly. "I'm flattered beyond measure."

"Well, if we're taking a hike tomorrow, I should probably get some sleep."

"Indeed. Georgia, may I ask you something before we turn in?"

"Anything."

"Why do you cry at the end of that movie? It's such a joyful, romantic ending. Are they happy tears?"

She took a breath. "Holly is my favorite character. I . . . I relate to her in a lot of ways. For her time, she was sort of a party girl, with lots of friends, endless male suitors, and this big exciting life. But she was also a woman who never unpacked the boxes in her apartment or named her cat, and I don't think she wanted to, or would let herself." She stopped and shook her head. "It's hard to explain, but those contradictions resonate deep in my soul. When she sings 'Moon River,' it hits me. I mean, Holly was right that people don't belong to each other. Yet at the end, when she lets go and gives in to love, the rain pounding down, well, it just gets me. I know it's silly. That's just movie magic."

He put his hand on hers. "Thank you for sharing that with me, and for watching your favorite film with me. I didn't mean to pry. It's just that your face while we were watching was so mesmerizing. I had to know what was behind that look in your eyes. And perhaps there's a bit of movie magic in real life too. I hope so at least."

"Roo, I know we just met, but I feel close to you."

He caressed her hand and gently said, "I feel the same." They smiled at one another, and he added, "Come on. I'll walk you up."

GEORGIA BOUNDED DOWNSTAIRS IN BLACK yoga pants, sneakers, and a white tank top with a sweatshirt jacket tied around her waist to find Roo waiting for her with two water bottles.

"You beat me," she said.

He smiled brightly. "Good morning. Shall we?"

She nodded and they headed out, crossing the street and walking toward the massive midnight-black volcano.

"Perhaps we should read this sign," Roo suggested. "Falling rocks. Blah blah blah. Narrow trail. Blah blah blah. Own risk." He turned to Georgia and said, "What do you say? Are you still game?"

"I say the last one to the top loses," she replied as she darted past him.

"A woman after my own heart," he said with a chuckle as he raced to catch up with her.

Soon they were nearly to the top, lost in conversation and the stark beauty surrounding them.

"I think Jean was really onto something. Looking around, this should be ugly in a way, yet it's spectacular," Roo commented.

"Maybe because it's not what we usually think of as beautiful. Don't you think there's something special when something or someone surprises you, and turns out to be more than you expected?"

"Indeed, I do," he replied, his eyes lingering on her

delicate face. "Uh, where did we leave off? I think it was my turn. What's your favorite color?"

"Red. I like things that are fiery, passionate," she said.

"Of course you do. Matches your personality. Mine is blue. Probably because I love the sea. Your turn."

"Favorite ice cream."

"Vanilla. But I always get different toppings, so don't write me off as boring."

Georgia smiled. "I never would. Mine is lemon or lime sorbet. In our world 'sorbet' is code for an actress who doesn't eat, but it's not that at all. I grew up with a lot of citrus trees, and I just like how refreshing it is on a hot day."

"There's so much pressure on women in our industry. Men just don't endure the same scrutiny. It's terribly unfair and makes me quite cross. It's like every decision a woman makes, even a flavor of ice cream, is subject to judgment."

"Thanks for saying that. Most guys don't get it at all. They don't even notice the double standards."

"I have quite a few friends who are actresses," Roo said. "And of course, my mum. We've always been close, and I've seen firsthand what she's had to deal with over the years. It's total rubbish. As a man I feel a responsibility to be aware of these things and try to improve conditions."

"You're a very sensitive, compassionate person," she remarked.

He smiled. "That's kind of you."

They were quiet for a moment before Georgia said, "Uh, it's your turn."

"Strangest thing you do when you're alone."

"I play guitar in my underwear."

"Excuse me?" he said, his eyes wide.

"I hang out at home nude or in my underwear, and sometimes I pick up my guitar and work on new music. Weird, right?"

"Uh, that may be the sexiest thing I ever heard. I'm blushing at the thought of it."

Georgia giggled. "What about you?"

"I make canned soup, cream of tomato or cream of celery, load it into a large bowl with a fistful of crackers, and watch documentaries on television. Could be about anything. Chernobyl. The Hindenburg. Creatures of the Amazon. Bird-watching. Whatever."

"Canned soup?" she said in a mocking tone.

"Funny how you got hung up on that. Thought I might be able to slip that past you with the bird-watching."

She laughed.

"Oddly, it relaxes me. What else can I say in my defense?"

"There's no need. I think it's sort of charming," she said.

"You do?"

"Oh yeah. You're surprising. I love that."

"Well, I like lots of other weird stuff. Canned sardines. Haggis. Liver and onions. Infomercials. Mops that can reach the ceiling. That's connected to my love of infomercials. Happy to go on if you find it endearing."

She laughed again. "You had me so distracted I didn't even realize. Look, we're just about at the top."

"Oh, wow," he said as they took the last few steps and reached the peak. "This is incredible."

"I've never seen anything like it," she said.

They fell silent, quietly looking around, taking in the view from every angle. Eventually Roo said, "You must be thirsty," and he handed her a water bottle.

"Thank you," she replied, and they both took a good drink. She pulled her phone out of her pocket and said, "We should take a selfie and try to capture the view."

"Please, allow me. Long arms," he said, taking the phone. "Being a tall, geeky, gangly thing in school is finally paying off."

She laughed and they took several photos. Then Georgia took the phone to take a few shots of the scenery. She insisted on taking a few of Roo as well. He held his arms up in a champion's pose. He then took a slew of pictures of Georgia, capturing her from every angle.

Eventually he said, "Well, I hate to ever leave, but we still must make it back down. I think we'll have worked up quite an appetite for breakfast."

"Yeah, I'm starving." She paused before adding, "Roo, this place is unforgettable. I'm glad I saw it with you."

He smiled. "I'm glad I saw it with you. Come on, last one to breakfast loses."

"THAT WAS SO GOOD," GEORGIA RAVED, scraping the last drop of her parfait. "Their homemade granola is delicious. I'm glad I asked them to add it to my usual."

"Yes, and since I got my eggs scrambled today with a side of sausage, we're not entirely creatures of habit, which is reassuring."

"Agreed. Besides, I was starving."

"Me too. A bit more tea?" he asked, lifting the pot.

She nodded. "Thank you."

"My pleasure. So, we certainly learned a lot about each other today. And yet . . ."

"Here I thought cream of celery soup was just something Andy Warhol painted. I never knew people actually eat it," she teased.

"We English don't exactly have a reputation for fine cuisine. Suppose I didn't do my countryfolk any favors sharing that little tidbit."

She giggled. "I'm sorry, I interrupted you. Opportunity to mock and all. What were you saying?"

"That we learned so much about each other, and yet I could ask you a million more questions."

"Such as?"

"You haven't mentioned a boyfriend. Are you seeing anyone?"

She shook her head.

"Seems impossible no one has scooped you up. I suppose there's a long line of those who try."

She looked down, blushing, and then stared straight into his eyes. "And you? Do you have . . ."

"A girlfriend? No." He paused for a moment before softly saying, "Georgia . . ." but was interrupted when Ástríður came into the room.

"May I get you two anything else? Some more tea?" she asked.

"Oh, I'm fine, thank you," Georgia replied.

"Me too. Thank you," Roo added.

Ástríður collected their dirty dishes and left.

"You were saying?" Georgia asked.

"Oh, uh, I was just going to ask what you plan to do the rest of the day?"

"I thought I'd just hang out in my room for a while. Catch up on my journaling. Maybe work on a new song I've been writing. And you?"

"The same. I've been feeling so inspired. I have an idea for a new play."

"That's great. Ready to head up?" she asked.

He nodded and they both rose. When they got upstairs, Georgia smiled and said, "Well, I guess I'll see you at dinner. Thanks for a great morning."

"Yes, thank you. Happy writing."

"Happy writing," she replied, turning toward her room as he turned toward his.

An hour later, Georgia was sitting in bed, strumming

her guitar. She was looking at the lyrics to a song scribbled in her notebook when, without thought, she started strumming the music to "Moon River" and began singing. Just as she finished the song, there was a light knock on the door.

She put her guitar down and went and opened the door to find Roo standing there.

"Hi, my huckleberry friend," he said sweetly.

"Hi," she said softly. "You heard me?"

"I came to see you and heard you playing. I couldn't help but to stand and listen. You have a lovely voice."

"Why did you come to see me?" she asked, staring into his eyes.

"Because I'm absolutely mad for you. Can't get more than two sentences down because you're all I can think about. If you feel the same . . ."

She took his hand and led him into her room, and he tapped the door shut.

He put his hand on her cheek, leaned forward, and kissed her softly. "My God," he whispered, "I've never felt anything like that."

He wove his fingers into her hair, and they began kissing passionately. Eventually, he pulled back and muttered, "Georgia, I want you so badly, but I don't want to screw this up by moving too fast, if you . . ."

"I want you too," she said, and she slipped her sundress over her head, standing before him in only a white thong, her wild spiral curls flowing freely.

"My God, you're so beautiful," he said as he began caressing the sides of her body. He started kissing her neck and slowly worked his way down to her breasts, gently licking her nipples as she moaned with delight. Roo continued planting kisses down her stomach, slowly pulled her underwear off, and put his mouth on her.

"Oh, Roo," she squealed. She touched his shoulders and he rose and pulled off his own clothes. "Take me," she whispered, and she guided him to the bed, lay down on her back, and he crawled on top of her. "You're spectacular," he said, and he slid inside of her, moving slowly, letting out moans of pleasure. "More, more," she whispered, grabbing his firm glutes as he began pounding into her before they both let out thunderous groans.

He lay beside her, stroking her cheek and kissing her tenderly, his body shaking. "That was mind-blowing. I've never felt anything like it. You're extraordinary and I'm absolutely bonkers mad for you."

She caressed the side of his face and pulled him up to the pillows, and they crawled under the blanket.

He stroked her cheek again and said, "I mean it. I'm crazy for you."

"I'm crazy for you too."

He kissed the tip of her nose, wrapped his arms around her, and said, "Let me snuggle you and we can take a little rest. I just want to hold you close to me."

They shut their eyes and fell asleep.

Two hours later, Georgia opened her eyes, still snug in Roo's arms. She turned toward him and he whispered, "Hello, darling."

"Hi."

"I'm so glad it wasn't a dream. Would have been the best dream of my life, but this is so much better."

She smiled. "I'm going to brush my teeth. I'll be right back."

"Promise?" he said.

"I promise," she said as she slipped out of bed.

"Just don't get dressed. You're too gorgeous for clothing."

She giggled and swayed her hips with exaggeration.

"Oh, you're killing me. You better hurry," he called.

When she returned, she said, "There's an extra toothbrush in the top drawer."

He jumped up, grazed her arm, and said, "Wait for me."

When he came back to the bedroom, she was gazing out the window. He ran his fingertips down her arm, took her hand, and said, "Come here, love."

Georgia turned to face him, and they started kissing heatedly. She began kissing his chest and working her way down, dropping to her knees, and taking him in her mouth. "Oh my God," he moaned. Roo held her head as she moved back and forth, and he moved in rhythm with her, his moans louder and louder. She rose, turned around, and leaned forward, her hands on the bed. He stood behind her, grabbed her hips, and slid into her gently, before he began thrusting. "More, more," she begged. He pounded harder and harder as she was screaming in ecstasy, until he exploded with bliss.

They both tried to catch their breath. Eventually, she turned to him and he scooped her up in his arms, carried her to the small love seat, and sat down with her in his lap. He looked at her with total adoration and said, "I could make love to you morning, noon, and night."

"Me too. My body is still trembling."

"Mine too."

"Do you want to spend the rest of the day here, with me?" she asked.

"Darling, I want to spend the rest of my life here with you, but today is a start."

They talked about their lives for hours. Georgia shared parts of her journal, which she had never done with anyone before. Roo told her about his new play in which "a man falls for an extraordinarily beautiful woman and becomes a bumbling fool because he can hardly speak around her."

After making love for a third time, Roo eventually said, "We should probably make ourselves presentable for dinner. But I was thinking later, if it's alright with you, perhaps I could get some of my things and stay with you."

"It's alright with me," she said.

He smiled. "Good. That makes it easier to tear myself out of your bed. Shall we have a shower before we head down?"

"Uh-huh. Roo, do you think Jean and Michael will know . . ."

"Yes, probably, I suppose. They usually get back from the set well before we had our last go-around, and we were quite loud, and the walls are quite thin."

"Oh," she said.

"Darling, please don't be embarrassed. I doubt they'll care very much, and we can be professional on set. Besides, I was haunted by our upcoming love scene. I couldn't imagine kissing you for the cameras when I so badly wanted to do it in private."

She smiled. "Let's shower." He kissed the tip of her nose and they started to get out of bed when she added, "I'm not embarrassed. I couldn't be embarrassed about being with you."

He smiled and said, "Come on, love."

Freshly showered and dressed, they bounded downstairs and found Jean and Michael in the dining room enjoying a cocktail. The two men started clapping when the young couple walked into the room.

"So, what have you two been up to? Make good use of your day off?" Michael asked.

"Rehearsing for your big scene perhaps?" Jean added, before bursting into laughter.

Georgia's face turned bright red.

Roo grabbed her hand and they sat at the table.

"You guys are terrible," Georgia said.

"Oh, relax. We're just teasing," Michael said. "We did the same thing to your folks after they hooked up. We teased them mercilessly. Look how that turned out. Thirty years later, they're still together. Probably a good omen for you two. Maybe you're following in their footsteps."

Roo smiled and slung his arm around Georgia. She smiled along for show, a lump in the shape of Michael's words forming in her throat.

CHAPTER 8

"You've been working nonstop for hours. Don't you want to take a break or at least stand up and stretch?" Betty asked, hovering in the bathroom doorway.

"Nope. I'm good," Khalil replied, wiping his brow.

"I feel so guilty that I roped you into helping me with my little DIY project on your first weekend off in ages, and now you're doing most of the work."

"Don't be silly. You were a powerhouse removing the old tiles. I should have known you'd be a badass with a ball-peen hammer and chisel. And it's a crime that someone can look so cute in safety goggles, not dorky like me." She giggled and he redirected his focus to the floor. "The surface is almost clean and ready. I think we should watch that YouTube video one more time before we attach the backer board and start installing the new tiles."

"We've seen it about a thousand times," she said with a laugh.

He turned to face her. "Since when are you against overpreparation? I remember when you had your first surgical procedure. You were in the skills lab all night. You stayed for hours even after you had perfected it."

"Yeah, well no one is going to be seriously harmed if the bathroom floor isn't tiled perfectly."

"Not true. My ego will never recover," he countered.

Betty laughed.

"Seriously, I just don't want to screw up your apartment. I know how careful you are. I'm sure you thought about this renovation for a long time before pulling the trigger. You spent ages selecting the tiles. The least I can do is try to make sure it comes out right. Give me a little while to finish prepping, and then we can watch the video. I promise, just one last time. Two tops."

"Okay. But after we install the tiles, let's order food. Clearly, I owe you dinner. You pick the cuisine."

"Sounds good."

Five hours later, they were sitting on Betty's couch opening Chinese takeout containers.

"Thank goodness we live in New York where you can get anything delivered anytime you want it," Betty remarked. "I can't believe how long that took."

"It's my fault. I wanted to make sure it was perfect."

"Well, it looks amazing. Huge upgrade. I just love the black and white. It's art deco and very New York."

Khalil smiled. "I'll come back tomorrow to help you add the grout and caulk."

"Oh, you don't have to. I already feel bad that I co-opted your Saturday for manual labor."

"Don't be silly. When I commit to something, I'm all in. Besides, I spend all my free time with you. What else am I going to do?"

"Thank you," she said softly, suddenly finding herself lingering on his chestnut-colored eyes.

"You're so welcome," he replied sweetly, staring back at her. In a barely audible voice, he said, "Betty, you . . ."

"Gee, I'm rattling on when you must be famished. You

haven't eaten anything since I tossed you that PowerBar hours ago. Please, help yourself," she said, gesturing at the takeout containers on the coffee table. "There are paper plates and chopsticks in that bag."

Betty uncorked a bottle of red wine and poured two glasses. "Cheers," she said, clinking her glass to his. "To my lifesaver."

"Cheers."

They each took some food and began eating.

"Holy cow," Khalil muttered. "I had no idea Chinese food could be so spicy."

"When you suggested Chinese, you said to get whatever. Those are a couple of my favorites: Szechuan chicken and hot and sour glass noodles. Is it too spicy?"

"Nah, it's okay," he gasped, chugging his bottled water.

"There's plain rice in that container," she said, gesturing. "That will help absorb the spice. Those veggies are steamed plain too, and the dumplings should be pretty mild if you don't like the heat."

"I just never knew Chinese food could be this spicy. It's even hotter than that five-alarm Thai food you brought us that time. My family always ordered lemon chicken and lo mein."

"Yeah, most people in this country are used to American Chinese food, which is often smothered in sweet sauces," Betty said. "My dad did a movie that filmed in China one summer when I was in high school, so we lived there for a couple months. I loved the food, especially from regions where they make things hot. My mom and sister both love spicy food, so we'd sort of challenge each other. Guess I got used to it. I was so excited when I moved to New York and was finally able to find those dishes again, done the authentic way."

"Did you always want to live in New York?" he asked.

"I applied to programs in Boston and New York. I guess I wanted to be somewhere . . ."—she paused as if searching for the right word—"serious. I wanted to be somewhere serious. Growing up in LA was great in a lot of ways, but there's a superficiality you can't escape, and a sort of carefree, whimsical attitude. It works for my family. My mom is totally boho. My dad and Georgia are actors. Albert's an artist and super low-key." She shook her head. "I don't want to come off sounding like a jerk. It's just so different from who I am. I like my feet planted firmly on the ground. I thought by coming to the Northeast I'd meet more people like me. And I have. I met you." Khalil smiled and she added, "New York has always been my favorite city, so when I was accepted it was a no-brainer."

"It's my favorite city too," he said.

"Were your parents disappointed that you didn't move back home after medical school?"

"Big time," Khalil replied. "My father was gutted. My parents' ophthalmology practice is only two miles from their house. My father always wanted me to set up a shingle next door. Being a small-time doctor in small-town middle America wasn't exactly my dream. It was a little rough trying to explain it to him. He felt like I was criticizing his choices, or looking down on him, when really I was just trying to explain they weren't my choices."

"I can see how that could be tough."

"The truth is I'm enormously grateful to him. In many ways, I wanted to be like him—his work ethic, drive, care for his patients, and he's always there for his family. There's no one I respect more than him, and of course my mother."

"How did your mother react when you decided to stay in New York?"

"She understood. She grew up in a city. Only moved to the boonies for my dad. It turns out it suits her. She loves working at a small local practice where you get to know your patients and their families. But my mom's worldly in her own way, different from my dad. Loves visiting me. She hasn't forgotten what city life is like. Plus, I think she's been hoping I'll meet someone and settle down. My folks met in their residency program, so . . ."

"She thought you might too."

He nodded. "It's not just my parents. Truthfully, I've always thought I'd end up with a fellow doctor. Common interests. Someone who understands the profession." His pace slowed as he spoke. "Someone with whom I could share everything. A partner."

The air suddenly felt thick as they sat, gazing at each other. Eventually, Khalil broke the silence. "I'm sorry. I'm rambling. You asked about my parents." Betty smiled sheepishly and took a sip of wine, her fair cheeks turning rosy, and he continued, "As an only child, I do feel bad sometimes that I don't live closer to them. I'm hoping to visit more once we finish our residency."

"It's hard to have much of a life outside of the hospital with our schedule."

"For two people who moved to New York because it's our favorite city, we really don't take advantage of it."

"Nonsense," she said, holding up the container of glass noodles. "This is very New York."

He smiled. "You know what I mean. We haven't seen much except the inside of the hospital and each other's apartments. We've been talking about going to a Broadway show forever, but . . ."

"We never do it. Always end up working."

"Hey, how about I check the schedule at the hospital and get tickets for the next night we both have off?" he proposed. "We could clean up, put on nice clothes, and see a show. Maybe even catch dinner beforehand. You know, like people do. I hear there are pretheater dinner specials all over Times Square."

Betty giggled. "You mean be like real people with a life, out in public?"

"Exactly."

"I'm in."

Khalil grinned from ear to ear, picked up his chopsticks, and took a bite of chicken. "Holy shit," he wheezed. "That's hot."

KHALIL PLACED THE WORD "XRAY" on the Scrabble board. "So, with the double letter score on *x* and the triple word score, that's sixty-six points for my little four-letter friend." He jumped up and began his silly victory dance, shaking his arms up in the air and moving his pelvis from side to side.

"You're the worst," Betty moaned, trying to suppress the smile creeping onto her face.

"I'm awesome," he protested, shimmying a few more times before plopping back on the couch with an air of triumph.

She took a pillow and playfully threw it at him.

"Don't be a sore loser," he said in a mocking tone.

"Don't be a bad winner," she countered with an exaggerated pout.

They burst into laughter. Then Khalil said, "It's late. I should probably go home. I'll come back in the morning to help you finish the bathroom floor."

Betty took a breath. "Seems silly for you to go back and forth, especially so late. I can set up the couch for you if you want to stay over. If you'd be comfortable."

"This couch is a lot better than the cot in the on-call lounge. Are you sure it isn't any trouble?"

"Of course not. Let me go grab the extra bedding."

Betty fixed the couch with sheets and a comforter. She fluffed the pillow and said, "There. You should be all set. I left an extra toothbrush out for you in the bathroom."

"Thank you."

"Well, good night."

"Good night."

She puttered to her bedroom, stopped at the doorway, and inadvertently turned to see Khalil pulling off his shirt. She found herself gazing at the contours of his back, his smooth dark skin, and his muscular arms. He started to turn, and she quickly hurried into the bedroom, closing the door behind her.

BETTY WOKE UP THE NEXT MORNING and lay in bed, feeling more rested than she had in a long time. Flashes of the night before popped into her mind: the effortless conversation during dinner, the Scrabble board covered with medical terms that she and Khalil both found hysterical although they joked that no one else would, the look on his face during his ridiculous victory dance, the arch of his back. A smile slid across her face, but as soon as she felt it, she shook her head to shoo away the unwanted feelings. During medical school she had learned how to distance herself from her emotions and used those skills frequently in all areas of life. Suddenly, she noticed the smell of coffee brewing and something else she couldn't discern. She stretched her arms and glanced over at the clock, stunned to see it was after ten. "I haven't slept that long in years," she muttered, slipping out of bed. She threw her robe on over her pajamas, brushed her teeth, and meandered out to the kitchen. Khalil was standing at the stove, gently stirring something in a sauté pan.

"Ah, you're up. Good morning," he said.

"Morning. I can't believe how late I slept."

"You needed to catch up."

"Seems you've been up for a while," she remarked.

"A few hours. I grabbed your key off the mail table and went out to get groceries. I'm making *shakshuka*. My mother's recipe. You got up just in time. I'm about to poach the eggs and then we can eat. There's coffee in the pot."

"Thank you," she said, pouring a mug for herself. She took a sip. "Ooh, that's good."

"Strong, right?"

"Uh-huh."

"I hate to admit it, but I've almost gotten used to the weak, bitter, barely palatable excuse for coffee at the hospital."

"Oh, I get it," Betty said. "Sometimes I actually miss that gross powdered cream substitute. I've gotten used to the artificial taste swirling with the staleness that coffee seems to have even when it's freshly brewed."

He smiled. "Okay, I'm dropping the eggs and then we can eat. Are you hungry?"

"Starving, but you really didn't need to go to this trouble. It's bad enough you've lost your weekend to my little home improvement project."

"It's no trouble." Khalil glanced back at her. "This is a great way to spend the weekend if you ask me."

She smiled as he turned away and started cracking the eggs in the fragrant green sauce.

"Can I do anything to help?" she asked.

"I bought a loaf of crusty bread. Maybe you could cut a couple slices."

"I'm on it."

Soon they were sitting at the table, eating.

"Mm," Betty moaned. "This is delicious."

"I'm glad you like it."

"Best breakfast I've had in ages."

He smiled. "I'll take the compliment even though I know I'm only competing with those lame PowerBars you normally have."

"Hey, don't mock the PowerBars. It's a meal on the go," she said with a sarcastic giggle.

"Speaking of being on the go, I checked out the Broadway sites while you were sleeping. Once I figure out when we both have a night off, I'll get tickets. What show do you want to see?"

"I'm up for anything. Your choice. Just let me know what I owe you."

"It's my treat."

"Well, then dinner will be on me," she insisted. "I'll find us one of those snazzy pretheater menus you mentioned."

He smiled and they continued eating.

"This is so incredibly good," she gushed.

"After we clean up, let's finish the bathroom floor. It's gorgeous out. If we get done early enough, maybe a run through Central Park?" he suggested.

"That sounds great."

"But I want to watch the YouTube video one more time. Just the last part. Don't be mad. I'm a bit of a perfectionist like you. Secretly you love that about me."

She smiled. They sat quietly eating for a few minutes before Betty looked up from her food and said, "You're right. This turned out to be a pretty great way to spend the weekend."

CHAPTER 9

"Strike!" Ryan declared as his bowling ball knocked down all the pins. He high-fived Albert and said, "You may be the king of laser tag, but I'm the king of candlepin bowling. You're up. It's your last turn, so make it count."

Albert selected a ball, lined himself up, moved forward, and released. He scrunched up his face as the ball flew into the gutter.

"Shake it off. Shake it off, Al," Ryan said, clapping his hands.

Albert grabbed another ball, took aim, and released it straight into the gutter. He turned toward Ryan and laughed, his face bright red.

"You've got this. You've got this," Ryan assured him, smiling and clapping. "The last one's always the charm."

Albert took another ball, stood at his mark, and then turned around, his back facing the bowling lane and his legs far apart. He winked at Ryan, shut his eyes, and then bent down and pushed the ball backward through his legs. He turned to watch as the ball rolled down the center of the lane and smashed into the pins, knocking eight over.

"Holy shit!" he said.

Ryan jumped up, hooting and hollering. Neither of them could stop laughing.

"Move of the night, Al. Bold. I may have won the game, but you won the night as far as I'm concerned."

Albert smiled. "Figured I couldn't be any worse if I literally wasn't even looking."

Ryan's phone beeped with a new text. He read it and said, "My friend Lucy's having some people over. She graduated a year ago. That was before you and I met, so I don't think you know her. She's this sweet, feisty little blogger chick with a pixie cut, kind of like Tinker Bell. Wanna go?" Albert looked a little unsure, so Ryan added, "It's just like seven or eight people. A small chill thing, all good friends of mine, all creative types. She's right over in Brookline. We could hop on the Green Line. We definitely shouldn't go hungry. Lucy's cupboards are either bare, or worse, she's cooked. What do you say we finish this pizza and stop by?"

"Sure."

THEY WERE ALL SITTING ON THE LIVING ROOM floor around the coffee table laughing hysterically after Lucy had convinced everyone to play with her Ouija board.

"I always suspected this place was haunted. My roommate never believed me. She's in for an earful when she gets home," Lucy said, her gold bangle bracelets clanking against each other as she ran her hand through her short brown hair. Albert had liked her right away when she greeted him with a hug, whispered, "Ryan is so crazy about you," and then launched into an overly personal story about her ex-boyfriend. Her friends were just as cool as she was—outrageous and kindhearted misfits. Ryan always fit in effortlessly, and on this night Albert felt like he did too.

"Okay, we've talked philosophy and politics, eaten that truly frightening dip Lucy made," Greg said, "and now we've communed with the spirit world. What's next?"

"Hey, that dip wasn't so bad," Lucy protested.

"Uh, it was chunky."

She threw a pillow at him. "We need someone with a talent to keep us occupied. Who can play an instrument or tell a really good ghost story?"

"Al can draw," Ryan volunteered.

Albert looked at him with trepidation.

Ryan whispered, "You're amazing." He refocused on the group. "He's crazy talented. He can do portraits, caricatures, superheroes, anything."

"Oh my God, I have the best idea. Al, will you do caricatures of us? But like, turn us into superheroes?" Lucy asked.

"Uh, yeah, sure. I don't have anything with me. Do you have paper and something to draw with?"

"I'll find stuff," Lucy said, springing up.

Albert turned to Ryan with nervous eyes.

"You've got this,' Ryan whispered, discreetly touching his arm. They smiled softly at each other, and Albert instantly felt more at ease.

Lucy returned with a large notebook of white paper and a handful of broken colored pencils. "Will this work?"

Albert nodded and took the supplies.

"Do me first," Lucy said, plopping down.

Albert smiled and began sketching, glancing up as Lucy smiled and posed, turning from side to side and making dramatic expressions. When he finished the caricature, he carefully ripped the paper out of the notebook and handed it to her.

"Wow!" she exclaimed. "Everyone, look at this. It's fucking brilliant."

There were oohs and aahs as the group marveled at the drawing. Albert had captured Lucy perfectly and transformed her into a modern version of Wonder Woman.

"Al, you're like super fucking talented. I don't say that to a lot of people," Lucy professed.

"Thanks," he replied, his cheeks rosy.

The others started clamoring for him to do their caricature next. Ryan sat beside him grinning from ear to ear as Albert handed out drawing after drawing. When each person had one, Ryan said, "Al, make one of yourself, as a superhero."

"Oh, that's okay. I . . ."

"Oh, you have to. Do it, Al," Lucy encouraged.

"Yeah, you need one too," Greg agreed.

Albert smiled bashfully and started drawing. When he finished, Ryan looked at the drawing and said, "That's awesome, Superboy."

They were gazing at each other when Lucy said, "These are so dope. I'm hanging mine up. Thanks, Al. Best party trick ever."

"Yeah, thanks," others chimed in.

"Any time," Albert replied, looking around at his new friends.

"LET MY BOYFRIEND GO," RYAN TEASED as they stood in the open doorway, Lucy hugging Albert again.

"Okay, party pooper," she whined, releasing Albert and saying to him, "Now I have your number in my cell to make sure we all hang this summer."

"Got it," Albert said.

"Catch you later, Luce. Thanks for the fun," Ryan said as he and Albert finally made their way out of the apartment. He turned to Albert. "They're the best, but that place can turn into a kind of vortex, especially when Lucy needs a distraction from her latest dating disaster."

"She's super nice. I like your friends a lot."

"They like you a lot too. Come on. There's someplace I want to take you," Ryan said as they bounded onto the street, inhaling the night air.

"Now?" Albert asked.

"Do you trust me?"

Albert nodded.

"Then come on."

They started walking down Beacon Street and Ryan said, "Everyone thought your art was sick. It made their night." Albert blushed and he continued, "Why'd you pick Superboy for yourself?"

"I don't know," Albert replied with a shrug. "It's just what popped into my mind."

"He's kind of tragic, the son of Superman."

"All superheroes are kind of tragic. That's what makes them interesting."

Ryan huffed. "You have a point. Never thought of it that way." He paused. "I didn't want to ask in front of everyone, but I recognized all the superheroes except the one you made for me. I loved it. Just didn't know who it was."

"It's one of my own. I created it just for you."

"You made me an original?" Ryan asked, his eyebrows raised.

"Yeah."

"Why?"

"Because you're not like anyone else."

Ryan smiled. "Neither are you."

After a quiet moment, Albert asked, "Are you going to tell me where we're going?"

"Hang a right up here." They started walking up the steep road lined with Tudor houses and Ryan said, "There's this really cool park. Up on the crest of the hill. When you're on the swings, you can see all of Boston."

"How do you know about it?"

"Discovered it my sophomore year. Lucy took me. After that, when I needed to escape, be alone, think, whatever, I'd hop on the T and go there. I haven't been since we graduated and moved to Cambridge, but we're nearby and I want you to see it."

Once they reached the top, Albert noticed a sign saying that the park closed after dusk. "Don't worry about that," Ryan said.

Albert followed him to the swings, not a soul in sight.

"You still trust me?" Ryan asked. Albert nodded and Ryan said, "Take a seat, shut your eyes, and I'll push you."

Albert obliged.

"Are your eyes shut?"

"Uh-huh."

"Keep them shut until I tell you to open them," Ryan instructed as he began pushing the swing.

Albert held onto the ropes on either side as he began to fly in the air. The higher and faster he went, the more boundless he felt. It was exhilarating. He could feel the swing reaching peak height when Ryan said, "Open your eyes."

Albert opened his eyes to see the sky bursting with stars and the Boston skyline illuminated before him. He was smiling so wide he couldn't speak as the swing kept taking him down and up, the city sparkling before him.

"Keep up the pace," Ryan said as he jumped on the swing beside him.

Soon they were swinging in unison. "Woo-hoo!" Ryan shouted.

Albert couldn't stop smiling. Eventually, they slowed down and dragged their feet on the ground until their swings stopped. They twisted to face each other, and Ryan said, "I just really wanted you to experience that. To feel like you're flying in the air, and the city you chose is before you, and you're so small and so big all at once, and everything is possible."

"Thank you for taking me here."

"You're welcome."

"Ryan . . ."

"Yeah?"

"I feel really comfortable with you. More than I have with anyone else."

"Me too."

They stared at each other for a moment and Ryan said, "There's no one here." He held out his hand and Albert took hold of it, and they sat quietly, underneath the starry midnight sky.

CHAPTER 10

Two months into the shoot, the cast was finishing dinner when Jean took the last swig of his bourbon and said, "We need to discuss the plan for our little excursion tomorrow morning." The actors listened as he continued, "We leave for Lake Mývatn at six o'clock sharp. Upon arrival, you'll head straight to wardrobe, hair, and makeup. I'll meet you there for notes since we're filming outdoors and there is no set. When you're ready, we start shooting. It's the most important scene in the film and I've scheduled one day for it, so we need to maximize our time when the lighting is right. I scoured the planet for the perfect location to create this cinematic moment. Someplace with otherworldly, nearly impossible beauty. Lake Mývatn is that place. Truth be told, I decided to shoot the entire film in Iceland just so we could travel there for this pivotal scene. You will be blown away. We'll also be photographing the poster for the film—the single image that will forever define it." Jean paused, his eyes suddenly looking far away.

"You okay there, old man?" Michael asked.

"Ah, yes," Jean said. "It suddenly occurred to me this will be the last time I photograph the poster image for a film."

"We're deeply honored to be a part of it," Roo said.

Georgia smiled compassionately and added, "You must be feeling so many mixed emotions."

Jean dismissively waved his hand in the air. "Rubbish. I just lost my way for a moment."

Georgia reached across the table and put her hand on his. "We can play that game if you want to, but if you're feeling a bit sentimental, or anything else, we're here to support you."

The trace of a smile flickered across Jean's wrinkled face. "You so remind me of your mother," he said, squeezing her hand. "She never lets me get away with any shit either." Georgia giggled and he continued, "But I'm fine, so save the drama for your performance."

The actors laughed.

"As I was saying, we'll be filming as long as the lighting allows. Then we'll be taken to a local inn to spend the night. Bring an overnight bag. I'm doing all the landscape shots the following day with the crew, driving back here the day after, so you'll get two days off. I can have you shuttled back here, or if you prefer you can spend your time off in the Mývatn area. There are mineral baths you may wish to visit, so pack swimwear."

"That sounds great. Thank you, Jean," Roo said.

"Well, I must retire. I'll see you bright and early. I'll be the one who looks like a corpse slurping an espresso," Jean groaned.

Georgia laughed, looked at him, and said, "I hope you know how much you mean to us, and how fucking brilliant we think you are."

He smirked and patted her hand. "Just like Ella indeed. Thank you, *ma chérie*."

"Come on, old man. I'll walk you up," Michael said, lending a hand.

Once they were gone, Roo slung his arm around Georgia and said, "Since we'll have a couple days off, how about we take my car tomorrow? That way we can go exploring during our free time. Check out the mineral baths. Go for a hike. Drive back leisurely."

"That sounds great."

"I'm glad I threw swim trunks in my luggage at the last minute. Did you bring a swimsuit? Wait, don't answer. That way I can picture you skinny-dipping, slipping into my arms, and well . . ."

She giggled.

"Darling, perhaps we should skip our usual movie night and head up to bed given the early departure time. Besides, now that I've given myself the image of you naked, I don't think I can wait to ravage you," he said.

She nodded, looked at him suggestively, and purred, "Let's go to bed."

THE NEXT MORNING, THE CAST AND CREW caravanned to the northern volcanic lake region. Roo and Georgia drove in his rental car, marveling at the landscape along the way, talking about their love of travel, and singing along to oldies on the radio. They were trailing a few minutes behind the others as they had to stop for gas. When they arrived at the location, they couldn't believe their eyes: stunning volcanic rock formations popping out of a shallow lake clear as glass surrounded by shamrock-colored greenery, with large grassy mounds in the shapes of swirls, volcanoes and mountains in the distance.

"Wow, Jean was right. It's utterly spectacular," Roo said.

"It looks like it's out of a storybook," Georgia remarked.

They smiled at each other, excited for the day, and opened their car doors. Just as they stepped outside, swarms of black insects swept in. There were so many it looked like sheets of blackness rolling through the sky.

"Oh my God," Georgia yelped, trying to protect her face and hair, with thousands of the small creatures swooping over them.

"Duck your head," Roo instructed as he covered his own head with both his arms, and they hurried to the wardrobe and makeup trailer. Roo opened the door and Georgia flew inside. She was frantically shaking her head and running her hands through her hair, trying to shake off the unwanted visitors.

"Ah, I see you've met the midges," Jean said.

"What on earth?" Georgia asked, still manically shaking out her long curls.

Jean snickered. "This place is named after swarms of small black flies called midges. They only live for seven days."

"You couldn't have mentioned this last night?" she said, shooing away the pests.

Jean nearly smiled. "Be glad we weren't here last month. That's their high season. They reach apocalyptic levels."

"It gets worse than this?" Georgia asked in disbelief.

Jean smiled ever so slightly. "Beauty always has another side. I quite love the midges. They are entirely harmless. To most, their presence here makes imperfect something that otherwise would be too perfect. These tragic little beings live such a short time yet perform such an important job during their brief blip on this planet. They are the protectors of pure, untouched beauty." He paused for a moment and added, "Sometimes the guardian of beauty is dark and ugly. Keeps things honest."

"That's so like you to say that," Michael said with a chuckle.

"Well, you coulda given a girl a warning. For you gentlemen, you throw a baseball cap on and call it a day. It's a bit more challenging for me," Georgia said, running her fingers through one curl at a time.

"Fair enough," Jean conceded.

"Here, let me help," Roo offered Georgia.

"While you do that, I'll review the part of the scene we'll be starting with," Jean said. "The old man is dying, and the two young lovers have taken him on an excursion for a picnic and to soak up the nature. As you know, I usually let you try things anyway you please. Not today. I've perfectly orchestrated the first shot. You must each be in precisely the right position. I can see it clearly. Michael standing in the back. Roo ten feet before him. Georgia ten feet before him. Both men are watching her, the most beautiful woman in the most beautiful setting, her long spiral curls cascading down her back. She walks ahead to look at some flowers and Michael approaches Roo. That's when he finally confronts him, and they have *the* conversation. Then, not knowing what has just transpired, Georgia turns to them, smiles, and waves them over. Does everyone understand?"

The actors nodded.

"I'll make sure your marks are clear. We'll be taking still photography shots too for the poster." Jean labored to his feet and said, "I'll leave you to get ready. Meet me on set."

Soon the actors ambled outside, Georgia wearing a long, flowing sundress in shades of green with speckles of yellow, her light brown curls spilling wildly all around. When she stepped into place, Jean muttered, "My God, see how she echoes the landscape. It is just as I imagined." A self-satisfied look danced in his eyes. He walked over to Michael, slightly adjusted his position, then did the same with Roo. When he approached Georgia, he whispered, "*Ma chérie*, you are perfection. Stay natural, just as you are."

She smiled at him, and he turned to the group and announced, "We are ready. Places, everyone." He made his way back to his director's chair and called, "Rolling . . . Action!"

Georgia stood, admiring the scenery, her lover admiring her, and his employer watching them both. Georgia took a couple steps forward and bent down to pick some flowers. Michael approached Roo, the two men standing side by side, both watching her.

"Are you enjoying the scenery?" Roo asked.

"Ah, yes. She is quite extraordinary," Michael replied. They stood for a moment, and he added, "I know you are lovers."

"We didn't mean for it to happen, but I won't deny it. She's the most beautiful woman I've ever met, in every way," Roo replied, adoration all over his face. He took a breath and said, "I know you have feelings for her."

"She brings me joy, pleasure," Michael said, his eyes still singularly focused forward. He let out a puff. "I have no romantic designs on her. I'm not a fool. I know she feels only pity for me."

"Compassion, not pity," Roo said, still looking ahead at Georgia picking flowers.

"I never had any intention of crossing any lines. The way I look at her, it is not sexual, as you see her. Trust me, it is something else entirely." Michael paused and said, "You have been digging into my books for months now. Haven't you figured out why I write about such darkness? Why I allow myself to be consumed by it?"

Roo shook his head ever so slightly. "I can only speculate."

Michael huffed. "I'll save you the trouble and give you the answer. You must bring people into the depths of darkness for them to appreciate the light, to even notice it. I have spent my life hunting for what she embodies in abundance. Now I wish to savor it for my few remaining days."

"What, exactly?" Roo asked, still looking straight ahead.

"Beauty. Pure beauty."

The men stood silently for a moment, watching Georgia. She rose with a small bouquet of flowers in her hand, turned toward them, smiled brightly, and waved them over. Both men smiled and, without looking at one another, began walking to her.

"Cut!" Jean hollered.

The actors turned to Jean, soft smiles on their faces as if they already knew it had been something special. He smirked and said, "Don't get too full of yourselves. Mother Nature did the heavy lifting. Let's do it again to capture it from different angles. Places, everyone."

AFTER A LONG DAY OF FILMING, JEAN AND the actors drove to the small local inn. Georgia and Roo unpacked in their room and then headed downstairs to meet Jean and Michael for dinner. They found Michael alone, sipping a cocktail.

"Where's Jean?" Georgia asked as she sat down.

"There's some kind of problem and he's outside speaking with a couple of the crew," Michael replied.

"What kind of problem?" Roo asked as he took the seat beside Georgia.

Michael shrugged.

"Today was magical. I hope he's pleased," Georgia said.

"You know by now he's not one to show his softer side, but I saw his face today. That was as close as he gets to being fucking ecstatic."

Georgia giggled.

Just then, Jean trudged into the room, grunting with frustration.

"What's wrong?" Michael asked as he helped Jean sit down.

"Some bloody weather event is coming. It's going to be pouring rain for the next two days. We won't be able to film the landscape shots until after the weather passes."

"Oh, no. That's a shame," Roo said.

"That's what I get for shooting a picture in this damn country. The weather can change on a whim, and she is unforgiving. They tell me when it rains here, it's relentless. There is no hope of filming on schedule."

"What are you going to do?" Michael asked.

"We can't go back and forth, it's too far, so we'll extend the location time here. I'll stay here and wait out the weather for the next two days, then we'll shoot the following day, and then return the day after that. So, looks like you'll all be off for the next four days. Actors are so bloody lucky. Directors get all the aggravation," he grumbled.

"I'm sorry, Jean," Georgia said. "If it's any consolation, you were right. This place is stunning. We all felt like we were a part of something magical today."

Jean huffed. "For the beautiful light we basked in today, the price is two days of rain. There is always an underside. Like those midges you so detested. The protectors of this land."

"The midges weren't so bad. Well, once the shock wore off," she said.

Two staff members came in to serve their dinner: local fish bathed in a langoustine sauce, with vegetables, potatoes, and homemade bread. They enjoyed their meal while talking about travel, art, and the glory days of location shoots. The actors praised Jean for making "real art" the "authentic way," to which he shrugged and snorted his responses. Jean began telling them a story about his first film but was interrupted when a crew member came into the room. "Mr. Mercier, we need to speak with you again, regarding some overtime issues with the locals we hired."

Jean sighed, leaned on the table for support, and labored to his feet. "I'll be back in a moment, I hope. Order me another bourbon."

Once he was out of earshot, Georgia said, "Gee, today was such an achievement for him. You could feel how cinematic and timeless those scenes will be. It's too bad he's not able to enjoy the incredible artistry he created."

"Honestly, I think he prefers to have something cosmic to gripe about. You know his shtick: there's always a dark side." Michael stopped to chuckle before adding, "Sometimes I think the universe does him favors by continually proving out his dystopian views."

Georgia and Roo laughed.

"On the plus side, we've all ended up with four days off," Michael noted.

"That's right," Roo said. He turned to Georgia and asked, "What do you think about a little adventure? Luckily, we have my car. We could take a trip somewhere."

"I'm always up for an adventure," she replied.

"How about the Blue Lagoon? I'm sure it's terribly romantic. We could leave after breakfast in the morning, stop along the way should we see something of interest, and be there sometime in the late afternoon."

"I'd love that. I've always wanted to go there."

Roo rubbed her arm as they smiled at each other. He turned to Michael. "There's plenty of room in the car if you'd like to come too. We can also drop you back off at the inn on the way if you prefer."

"Thanks, but I'm gonna stay here with the old man. He may be able to use some assistance. I don't want to leave him on his own."

"That's kind of you. The way you look out for him," Georgia said.

Michael shrugged. "He's been good to me."

"Well, if you don't mind, I think we'll go upstairs and get some rest so we can get an early start tomorrow," Georgia said. "Will you tell Jean we said good night?"

Michael nodded.

Georgia walked over and leaned down to give him a hug. "You're a good guy, Michael Hennesey. Don't worry, I won't tell anyone."

"They'd never believe you anyway," he replied with a chuckle.

The young couple excused themselves, and Michael ordered another round of drinks for himself and Jean. Soon Jean returned and took his seat.

"Everything alright?" Michael asked.

Jean huffed. "Right as rain. Quite literally." He took a sip of his drink and asked, "Where are our young star-crossed lovers?"

"Star-crossed? More like written in the stars," Michael said.

Jean smiled softly. "Indeed, you are right about that."

"They decided to take a trip to the Blue Lagoon tomorrow for a romantic getaway, so they wanted to get to bed early."

"Ah."

"So, while we're alone, I've been dying to tell you that I've got your number, old man."

Jean furrowed his brow.

"I know what the film is really about," Michael explained. "I actually figured it out the first week, but one can never be certain with you. After today, it became clear I was right all along."

"Do tell," Jean said skeptically.

"It's about *you*," Michael declared. "It's your autobiography."

Jean smirked. "Go on."

"You're the controversial, reclusive artist who's dying. This film is your way of setting the record straight, or perhaps amusing yourself and giving your critics the finger." Jean laughed and Michael continued, "I couldn't believe it when I realized I was playing some version of you. Talk about pressure. Plus, you could have any actor you want. Don't get me wrong, I'm honored but also kind of flabbergasted. Why'd you choose me?"

"I'm not one to wax on prophetically about my body of work, but *Celebration* has always been special to me. The film. The summer we all spent together shooting it. Better than anything else, it represents my work, and my work represents me. This made you the natural choice." Michael started to smile just as Jean added, "Besides, you were a real shit back then, navel-gazing, womanizing, self-aggrandizing. Let's just say, it made you the ideal choice to play a twisted fucker like me."

Never one to take things too seriously, Michael laughed. "Aw shucks, I'm flattered."

Jean shrugged.

"There's more I've figured out about the film," Michael said, taking a swig of his drink.

"Oh," Jean said.

Michael nodded. "The film is about your search for beauty through your art, underneath all the dark and depressing stuff. You picked this location because of the midges. When you were telling Georgia about them, you said, 'Sometimes the guardian of beauty is dark and ugly.' You were talking about yourself. The landscape is like the fourth character in the film because it's a metaphor for how you understand your role as an artist, as a truth teller. You need to go dark so that others may see the light."

"I liked you better when you were shallow and vapid."

Michael laughed. "Oh, and I'm not done. There is one thing I couldn't quite figure out until today. Georgia's role in the film. It's no secret she looks just like Ella."

Jean glanced down and then back at Michael. "Georgia is a fine actress."

"She is. Gifted, I think. But that's not why you hired her. The old man is in love with her." He paused before continuing. "The movie is about the only woman you've ever truly loved: Ella. For fuck's sake, you named the character Giselle. Uh, not that far off from Gabriella." Michael took a swill of his drink, looking proud of himself.

"See, bravado will always catch up to you, *mon ami*." Jean ran his finger around the rim of his glass. "You are right, Georgia's character is meant to be Ella, the most beautiful woman I have ever known. But you weren't paying attention to your own lines today. The old man is not in love with her. To him, she is the embodiment of beauty. She is a symbol for all the beauty in the world. It is not romantic. Nor are my feelings for Ella. But when I think about pure beauty in this wasteland of human shit, I think about the way her hair moves in the breeze, the arch of her back, the curve of her lips when she smiles, the gleam in her eyes when she says something irreverent and brilliant. The film is not about a man's search for love. It is about his acceptance that we live in a swampland of suffering and despair, and yet, amidst it, there will always be beauty. It can penetrate even the darkest places. Even the darkest of hearts, such as his own."

Michael ran his hand through his hair. "Well, that's some heavy shit."

"Heavy shit indeed," Jean agreed.

Michael raised his glass and said, "I am truly honored you trusted me with the part."

Jean nodded. "You haven't fucked it up yet."

Michael laughed. "For the record, I don't think the old man's heart is as dark as he pretends." He took the last swig of his drink and added, "But I'll keep this all between us, Jean. I don't think Finn will buy that load of crap that you don't have the fucking hots for his wife."

CHAPTER 11

"Wow, it's like we're on the moon or something," Georgia remarked as they drove down the road leading to the Blue Lagoon, nothing but endless vistas of lava rocks all around them as far as the eye could see.

"It's wild. We're almost there," Roo said.

"I can't believe how long it took. It's been over eight hours," Georgia said.

"Well, it would have been more like six and a half if we hadn't stopped so much along the way."

"That's the best part of a road trip," she replied. "All the cool little spots you see along the way. We took so many gorgeous photos."

"Not to mention souvenirs. That Icelandic tourism book has some tips for visiting the lagoon, and one simply can't leave Iceland without the requisite shot glass. The shawl you bought is lovely. You're the only woman I've ever known who could drape herself in wool and make it look so sexy." She giggled and he continued, "I must say I also quite enjoyed those sandwiches we picked up in that tiny little town. Who knew smoked lamb was so delicious?"

Georgia smiled. "Oh, look. There's steam up ahead. We must be getting close."

"There were three hotel options and we're staying at the swankiest, but I was only able to book a regular room, not one of their palatial suites."

"I'm sure it'll be great. Besides, we've been cozy in my little room at the inn all summer," she replied, rubbing his arm. "In case you haven't figured it out, I'm a girl who can pretty much go anywhere with a backpack and a sleeping bag."

"Is that so?" he asked skeptically.

"Well, the backpack yes, although I do have a tendency to overstuff it. I admit a fondness for indoor plumbing, shampoo, and a good mattress, but I can make do."

"Me too. The truth is, I suppose I could make do with anything as long as you're there."

They smiled at each other as Roo pulled up to the front of the luxurious five-star Retreat Hotel. Young men in uniform quickly opened their doors and ushered them inside, assuring them the luggage was following.

"This is so beautiful," Georgia remarked, looking around the modern lobby with a wall of windows facing the lagoon and rolling moss-covered chocolate-brown mountains in the distance.

A woman came rushing over from the reception desk. "Welcome, Mr. Reed and Ms. Forrester. Please, have a seat anywhere." They sat down on one of the many couches and the woman continued, "I understand this is your first visit. May I offer you something to drink? Water? Champagne? Tea or coffee?"

"Ooh, champagne would be nice," Georgia said.

"For me as well," Roo added.

"Certainly. Please excuse me for a moment. While I'm gone, you can look over this itinerary," she said, handing a printout to Roo. "I've booked you dinner at Lava at eight o'clock, in case you'd like to take a dip in the lagoon first. I've taken the liberty of booking a couples massage tomorrow, as well as additional dinners. We can schedule anything else or cancel anything on your behalf. Full spa services and other activities are printed on the last page. Also, you'll want to put these bracelets on—they give you access to your room, the spa, the lagoon, and can be used to charge things to your account."

"Thank you," Roo said.

"Our afternoon tea just ended, but if you're hungry, I'm sure I could get you a few canapés and sweets to go with your champagne."

"I'm fine. Thank you, though," Georgia said.

"Yes, I'll save room for dinner," Roo concurred.

As soon as she was out of earshot, Georgia gushed, "This place seems amazing."

Roo slung his arm around her and said, "Look at this list. Morning yoga, a full breakfast, wine tastings, high tea, loads of spa services, and the lagoon itself."

"Oh, I want to see if I can book a facial."

Their host returned and handed them each a flute.

"Cheers, darling," Roo said, clinking his glass to hers.

"Cheers."

AFTER A TOUR OF THE FACILITIES, GEORGIA and Roo went to their room, which featured a view of moss-covered lava rocks, the lagoon water trickling by. Roo noticed the freestanding bathtub facing the wall of windows and remarked, "We'll definitely have to take a soak in this. Doesn't get more romantic."

Georgia giggled. "There's also a rainfall shower with room for two."

"I like the sound of that," he replied, slipping his arms around her waist and staring adoringly into her eyes. "So, what shall we do first?"

"The lagoon!" she squealed.

He smiled. "I love how excited you get for something new. Your spirit is so alive, it's infectious."

"Come on, let's change into our swimsuits," she said, tugging his hand.

Soon Roo was in blue swim trunks and Georgia in a white string bikini. She was looking in the bathroom mirror and pulling her long curls into a bun when Roo slipped his hands around her waist, gently kissed her shoulder, and whispered, "You are extraordinarily beautiful and damn sexy."

She finished fixing her hair, turned to face him, and said, "You're not so bad either."

They kissed softly and Roo said, "If we want to make it to the lagoon, I don't think we can do that again, not with you looking like this. You are a goddess."

She giggled. "Come on, let's put on our matching white robes and flip-flops and head over."

Soon they were walking down the stairs of the spa that led into the private part of the lagoon reserved for hotel guests.

"Wow, it's as warm as a bath," Georgia said as they stepped into the milky blue water. "The color is incredible. I've never seen anything like it."

"Follow me," Roo said, and he used his bracelet to open a small see-through door, which led into the open-air part of the lagoon.

"Oh, wow!" Georgia exclaimed. They wandered through the mineral-rich water, encased between mounds of lava rocks. Steam rose around them as they found themselves shoulder-deep, not a soul in sight. "The ground is soft and a little squishy," she remarked.

"It's a kind of white mud. This whole thing comes from silica, a product of lava. It's mixed with geothermal seawater in volcanic aquifers deep underground, which gives the lagoon its mineral properties, temperature, and iconic coloring," Roo explained.

"I'm impressed," Georgia said.

"Don't be. I was reading the tourism book while you were changing. That's the extent of what I learned."

"How about we sit over here, on this ledge?" Georgia suggested.

They sat down in the far corner of the private lagoon.

"This is paradise," Roo said as he draped his arm around Georgia.

She sighed contentedly. "Absolute bliss."

"Georgia . . ."

"Yes?" she said, looking at him.

"It's paradise because I'm with you." He took a moment to just gaze into her eyes. "I love you. I'm madly in love with you."

"Oh, Roo." She gently pressed her mouth to his, looked back into his eyes, and said, "I love you too."

He grinned from ear to ear. "I've wanted to say it for so long. Since the first time we made love. Honestly, I already knew I loved you when I showed up at your door that day."

"And here I thought you just wanted to see if you could catch me playing guitar in the nude."

He laughed. "Well, there was that, of course. But I had fallen in love with you, Georgia. In my heart, I believe we're soulmates." He stroked her cheek and kissed her. "You've made me so happy. Knowing you love me too, it's everything I could hope for."

"I do love you." She paused and said, "Roo . . ."

"What, my darling?"

"I've never said that to anyone before. I mean, I've never been in love."

"Me either. I was hoping to only do it once."

"I wasn't looking for a relationship or love."

"Me either," he said. He kissed the tip of her nose and added, "But it found us anyway."

They rested their foreheads together for an intimate moment.

"I do so love you, darling," he said.

"I love you."

They started to kiss but were interrupted when a bikini-clad woman holding a phone walked by on one of the surrounding bridges and in a thick Icelandic accent said, "Sorry to sneak up on you. I work at the resort, taking pictures of guests in the lagoon. It's a complimentary service we offer. Would you like your photo taken?"

"We would love that!" Georgia enthused.

The couple posed for several photos. In the last one, Roo had his arm around Georgia and was kissing her cheek as she smiled widely.

Roo gave the photographer his email address and she promised to send the photos. Before she left, Georgia asked, "Is your job really to hang out in the lagoon all day taking photos of tourists?"

"Yes," she replied.

"You may have the actual best job in the world," Georgia said.

"I know," she replied with a smile before leaving the couple to themselves.

Georgia turned to Roo and said, "I thought we were lucky to be actors, but she's got it made. If she ever retires, maybe I can apply for her job."

"No fair. I wanted it."

"Sorry. I don't think you'll look as good in a bikini, which seems to be the required uniform."

"Speaking of which," he said, running his hands down her body and nibbling her earlobe, "It's torture looking at you in this tiny thing. I'm looking forward to taking it off you in our fabulous two-person shower."

After a relaxing soak in the lagoon, they shuffled back to their room, hand in hand. Georgia released her long locks, and then without a word, they took off their robes and flip-flops and got into the shower, turning on the rainfall.

"Here, let me help you," Georgia said, slipping her hands beneath his waistband and peeling off his swimsuit.

"Allow me to return the favor," he said, untying her bikini top and watching it fall to the floor before kneeling down and pulling off her bathing suit bottom.

He rose, wove his fingers into her hair, and began kissing her passionately. "I've never felt this way," he whispered, kissing her ear, neck, and moving back to her mouth, while caressing her breasts.

"Me neither," she purred, slipping her hands below his waist. "I want you so badly and I feel how much you want me."

"I do," he whispered. He turned her around, slipped his hand between her legs, and started moving his fingers in a circular motion, kissing her neck and shoulder. She began to moan and writhe around in delight.

"That's it, love," he whispered, as her moans became louder and louder.

"Take me," she begged, and he slid inside of her, gently moving back and forth, as they both groaned. He moved faster and faster until they both yelped with pleasure.

His quaking body pressed to hers, Roo kissed her shoulder and rubbed her arms. A moment passed as they caught their breath, and he gently turned her to face him. He caressed the side of her face and whispered, "I love you. I'm so lost in you, and found at the same time. I've never felt anything like it. You're my soulmate and I'll love you forever."

Georgia kissed him softly. "Come on, let's finish washing up so we can go to a romantic dinner."

CINEMATIC DESTINIES

THE NEXT DAY, THEY ENJOYED MORNING yoga, a huge breakfast spread that included smoothies, smoked salmon, cheese, fruit, and poached eggs, followed by facials, a couples massage, a light lunch of local sushi and ceviche, and a long dip in the lagoon. After savoring an artfully prepared tasting menu at Moss, the resort's most upscale restaurant, they meandered back to their room.

"That meal was beyond words, but I'm so full," Georgia said.

"Shall we sit outside on the patio, get some fresh air?" Roo asked.

Georgia nodded. She grabbed her new hunter-green wool shawl and wrapped it around her shoulders, and they ambled to the patio.

"My God, you have the most exquisite green eyes. You really are the only woman I've ever known who could look as sexy wrapped in wool as she does in a bikini," Roo gushed.

Georgia blushed. "Let's sit together in the cocoon chair," she suggested.

Roo sat down, then Georgia. He wrapped his arms around her, and she rested her feet on a small ottoman. He dropped a kiss in her hair and said, "This is so relaxing. It's hard to imagine feeling any better than I do right now."

"I hope we don't end up too relaxed, if that's a thing. We kind of zombied out today with all the spa stuff," she said.

"We could change it up. We're not that far from Reykjavík. Maybe tomorrow afternoon we could drive into the city, poke around the shops, pick up more souvenirs, grab dinner somewhere."

"Ooh, that sounds like fun. I've heard Reykjavík is known for its nightlife."

"Then perhaps we'll have to check out a pub after dinner," he suggested.

"That sounds great." They sat quietly for a moment,

and she said, "This view is mesmerizing. I don't think I'll ever stop feeling like we're on another planet."

"It is transporting," Roo agreed. "I was looking through our trusty little guidebook. Seems there are some hiking trails around here. I'm sure we could get more information. Perhaps tomorrow after breakfast we could go exploring. It will be our last full day here. Would be a pity not to take it all in."

"That sounds great. I can't get enough of this view," Georgia replied.

"Well, that's a shame. I hope you can tear yourself away because I've just got to get you inside. I'm compelled to make love with you all night."

"In that case, let's go to bed."

GEORGIA WAS SIPPING THE LAST OF HER morning tea when Roo scurried back from the reception desk and said, "I have the perfect hike for us. There's what they call a forest at the base of that mountain, really just a small stretch of pine trees or something," he said, pointing to the window. "The forest is called Selskógur, but since there are no other trees for miles, some of the locals call it 'The Magical Little Forest.' Apparently, there are songbirds and wild rabbits that inhabit it. To get there, you walk through an area of the lagoon that's not open for use but is supposed to be gorgeous for photography, and then you continue on a path through the fields of lava rocks. I think it would take about an hour and a half to walk there and back, of course longer for us no doubt if we stop to take photos. What do you think?"

"It sounds perfect," she said. "Let's go."

An hour later, they arrived at the forest.

"Yay!" Georgia yelled, twirling around. "We made it."

"That was the single most unusual hike of my life. You were spot-on saying it was like walking on the moon, through paths of craters. Completely surreal."

"You know what's kind of surreal?" she said, waving her arms around. "This small little clump of trees is considered a forest here. It's so strange. Yet somehow it seems beautiful. I don't think I'd feel as satisfied making it to the finish line of a race as I did making it here."

He smiled. "Because trees are so scarce it seems special, miraculous."

"I believe the word is *magical*," she said with a playful look.

"Indeed."

"Oh look," Georgia said, pointing. "There really are rabbits."

"Ah, and songbirds too," Roo added, a few birds beginning to chirp as if on cue. "This place is like a fairy tale of sorts."

Georgia giggled. "It's kind of funny. My mother wrote some children's fairy-tale books. They all take place in a forest that I kind of pictured like this one."

"I didn't know that about your mother. I was only aware of her philosophy books."

"She wrote a really famous philosophy book about love, dedicated to my dad, of course. After that, she decided to share her views in a kid-friendly format, I think as an alternative to traditional princess stories. She wrote the books when I was little and dedicated them to me and my siblings."

"That's so special. Did you like them?" he asked.

She nodded. "I loved them when I was little. They all took place somewhere like this. I don't remember the details, but at the end of one of them, the characters look up at the top of the trees, trying to figure out where the trees end and the sky begins. Eventually, they decide it doesn't matter. That's when they realize how beautiful it is." She craned her neck to look at the top of the trees and added, "It was a metaphor about love, and how we try to hold on to ourselves, but if we let go, we create something new with another person—like the space where the trees touch the sky."

"That's lovely."

Georgia shrugged. "My mom's a hopeless romantic. I've never taken it too seriously. It's a nice story, though."

He gave her a gentle peck on the lips. "You never know, maybe it's more than a nice story."

"Do you really believe in those kinds of fairy tales?"

Two songbirds began singing, again as if on cue. Roo smiled and said, "More so by the minute."

"THAT PLACE? ARE YOU QUITE SURE?" Roo asked.

"Yes, let's get in line," Georgia replied, tugging his hand.

He laughed. "Here I'd take you to the best restaurant in the city, and you choose this little hole-in-the-wall crêperie where we have to wait in a line spilling out the door."

"The line means it's good. Besides, we did fancy last night. Don't you just love crêpes?"

He kissed her forehead. "I do. Honestly, this place would probably be my pick too, I just didn't know it would be yours. You are surprising, Georgia Sinclair Forrester."

"Good. I don't want you to get bored."

"No chance of that," he assured her.

"Reykjavík is so cool. Although I'm still bummed out that the penis museum was closed. What kinds of exhibits do you suppose they have?"

"I don't know," he said, "but I'm glad we missed our chance. I'm afraid you'd see I don't measure up and that you could do a lot better."

She giggled and refocused on the crêperie as they moved forward in line. "This place is going to be awesome."

"It bloody well smells good. What are you going to have in yours, something savory or something sweet?"

"I'm not sure," she replied, reading the menu posted in the window. "I kind of have a sweet tooth right now, but it is supposed to be our dinner."

"How about we get one of each and share, then we won't have to feel guilty," Roo suggested.

"That sounds like a perfect plan. What fillings do you like?"

"I'm easy. I'll eat just about anything. Like I've told you, my pantry at home is mostly tins and cans, and I don't mind a bit." She giggled and he asked, "Do you fancy ham and cheese?"

"Yeah. Maybe we can add some spinach to make it a little healthier."

"And for the sweet one?" he asked.

"Hmm. I can't decide between strawberries and whipped cream, which we can kinda sorta pretend is healthy, or dark chocolate with a scoop of pistachio gelato. Which do you prefer?"

"Let's get both and share. I'm famished anyway."

"You're naughty. I like it."

He smiled. "Oh, those people at that back table are leaving. Try to snag it while I order."

She snaked through the narrow, crowded space and grabbed the table, admiring the surrealist paintings hanging on the walls.

Soon Roo joined her with their food and two glasses of water and said, "Let's dig in."

As they scraped the last bites of the chocolate-and-pistachio crêpe, Georgia gestured and said, "You've got a bit of melted chocolate on your lips."

He used a napkin to wipe his mouth. "Can't take me anywhere. That one was the winner."

She nodded and drank the rest of her water. "Silly as it sounds, one of the things I'm going to miss the most is the Icelandic water. It's so pure. I'm so over the bottled water thing in LA."

"Yes, there's much I'll miss," he said. They were quiet for a moment, and he added, "When we return tomorrow, there will only be a few weeks left of filming."

"Yeah, I've been thinking about that too."

"Georgia, I realize that our relationship has happened quickly and we're still learning about each other, but I'm certain of my feelings for you. At the risk of scaring the hell out of you, there's something I must tell you." She raised her eyebrows and he continued, "I want to spend the rest of my life with you. Honestly, I can't imagine living without you, or at least I don't want to. I know it's fast and whirlwind, but in my heart, I feel we're meant for each other. Soulmates. That's forever. I don't know what your plans are for when the shoot ends, but I hope they include me."

"I don't know what to say. I love you too, but . . ."

"What?" he said, reaching his hand across the table and taking hold of hers. "It's okay. Tell me how you're feeling."

She took a breath. "I'm feeling like I can't imagine being without you either, and I don't have any plans after the film, but I don't know what any of that means. I've never even really had a boyfriend before. I'm not good at that stuff. This is new to me."

"Is it really true you've never had a boyfriend?"

Georgia nodded. "I had a couple in high school that lasted like a month, and I've had casual things with lots of guys. Affairs, basically. I was never interested in anything else. Have you had lots of girlfriends?"

"I had a couple that were serious, but I never felt for them as I feel for you."

"Do you have plans after the shoot?" she asked.

Roo shook his head. "I want to make plans with you."

"I'm not much of a planner. I'm pretty spontaneous."

"I know, darling," he said with a smile. "It's one of the things I adore about you. What if after we wrap the film, we take a little time to explore more of Iceland? Put that guidebook to good use. Then we can decide what's next. One adventure at a time. Do you like that idea?"

"Yes. It sounds perfect." They sat for a moment smiling at each other before Georgia said, "Now come on, let's go find a pub and party into the wee hours."

THE NEXT MORNING, GEORGIA OPENED HER eyes, her nude limbs entangled in Roo's. She craned her neck to see what time it was, and he woke up.

"Morning," he said softly.

"Sorry I woke you."

"That's alright. What time is it?"

"A little after eight."

Roo stretched his arms and yawned. "We should probably get breakfast so there's time for a last dip in the lagoon before checkout."

"Roo . . ."

"What is it, love? You look like something's on your mind."

"It's just what you said last night, about wanting to be together after the film, and that you'll always . . ."

"Love you? Yes. What about it?"

"I just don't want to disappoint you," she said. "I mean, we've been in this exotic place, making this film where we're lovers and . . ."

"Oh darling, do you fear it's just some kind of affair that happens on location, and we'll feel differently in our real lives?"

"The thing is, this *is* my real life. Traveling from place to place, making films, not knowing what comes next. There's no other life I'm returning to."

He smiled. "Your adventurous spirit may be my favorite thing about you. Or perhaps it's this," he said, caressing her hair. "Or this," he continued, running his fingers down her arm. "Or maybe it's this," he said, leaning forward and kissing her. When he pulled back, he whispered, "Georgia, I'm in love with you, only you, forever you. Tell me you feel the same."

"I do."

"Then there's nothing to fear. We'll figure it out. Okay?"

She nodded.

"Good, then let's throw something on and get breakfast. I'm starving. Are you hungry?"

"Yeah."

They slipped out of bed; all the while Georgia tried to convince herself that the pit in her stomach was hunger and not fear.

CHAPTER 12

Betty staggered into her apartment after her morning run through the park. She turned the coffee pot on, jumped in the shower, and got ready for work. A steaming mug of coffee in hand, she surveyed her closet, trying to select an outfit to bring for that evening. "Hmm, maybe this," she muttered, pulling out a simple navy-blue wrap dress. "But which shoes would go? Maybe I should just wear jeans and call it a day." After spending ten minutes pulling out outfits only to put them back, she decided to FaceTime Georgia.

"Well, this is a surprise," Georgia answered, lounging on the couch in her trailer. "Oh my God, did you see the latest texts from Mom and Dad? Seems like they went from Bali to Paris. What a whirlwind adventure. That picture of them in front of the Eiffel Tower is kind of adorable. Guess it's Saint-Tropez next."

"Yeah, I saw. They look so happy. That reminds me, I've been meaning to text you and Albert. We should really decide on an anniversary gift for them. I was thinking it might be nice to ask their close friends to send us little videos wishing them happy anniversary. I'm sure Al could edit them together."

"Great idea. They'll love it," Georgia said.

"I'll contact their friends, but can you ask Jean and Michael?"

"Sure thing. So, is that why you called?"

"I'm trying to pick an outfit for tonight and I need help," Betty explained. "Is it a bad time?"

"No. I'm just chilling while they set up the next shot."

"Good, because I've got to be out of here in ten minutes to make my shift."

"Don't sweat it. I'm your girl. Where are you going tonight?"

"Dinner and a Broadway show. Honestly, it's been so long since I've been anywhere that I think I've forgotten how humans dress."

"Who are you going with?" Georgia asked.

"Khalil."

"*Ooh*, it's a date with your boyfriend."

"He's *not* my boyfriend," Betty insisted.

"Saturday night, dinner and theater? Sounds like a date to me."

"Well, you'd be wrong."

"Is he picking you up?"

"He's meeting me at the hospital. He has the day off and I have to work, so . . ."

"So, he's picking you up. How chivalrous," Georgia said with a mischievous giggle.

Betty rolled her eyes. "I don't have time for this. Are you going to help me or not?"

"Yes, chill. I'm just teasing you. Show me the outfits you're considering."

Betty obliged, pulling out one hanger after another, to which Georgia emphatically said, "No," each time.

"You can't veto everything," Betty moaned.

"God, sis, when was the last time you went shopping? You're twenty-eight, not forty-eight. Ditch the little sweater ensembles pronto, like the second we hang up. Donate them to charity or something."

Betty sighed. "Maybe I should just wear jeans. That's my go-to when I'm not in scrubs."

"It's Saturday night in New York City. Put on something that makes you feel pretty. Come on, you must have a cute dress tucked away."

Betty pulled out the knee-length navy-blue wrap dress. "What about this?"

"Ooh, that's nice. Chic, understated, and a little flirty."

"Georgia, I told you it's not a date and . . ."

"I'm just saying you'll look and feel great."

"I don't know what shoes to wear," Betty complained.

"Show me what you've got."

Betty scanned the phone over her shoe rack until Georgia said, "Those. The nude ballet flats. That's a perfect outfit. And sis, do your hair and put on a little makeup. A ponytail in a scrunchie doesn't exactly scream Saturday night in New York."

Betty rolled her eyes. "Thanks for your help. Well, sort of."

"Anytime. Before you go, tell me one thing." Betty raised her eyebrows and Georgia continued, "If he's just a friend, why so stressed about your outfit?" After a moment of silence, Georgia said, "Exactly."

"You are a pain in the ass. Gotta go. Thanks for your help."

"Have fun on your date," Georgia said, just before Betty ended the call.

Betty shook her head and muttered, "That's what you get for calling her." She packed her dress and shoes and was about to run out the door, but she hesitated and ran back to grab her hairbrush and makeup bag.

AFTER FINISHING ROUNDS, BETTY WAS HEADING to the lounge to change when her attending physician caught up with her. "Forrester, there's a trauma coming in. I know your shift just ended, but I want you in on this."

"But . . ."

"A woman pregnant with twins was in a car crash. The EMTs reported that she went into labor. I need all hands on deck, plus it would be a good learning experience. If you can't stay, tell me now and I'll page O'Brian."

Betty took a breath. "Of course I'll stay."

"Meet me in labor and delivery."

Betty nodded. She hurried down the hallway to the residents' lounge. When she opened the door, she saw Khalil waiting for her, looking handsome in black slacks and a button-down shirt that accentuated his muscular physique. He beamed at the sight of her. "Hey, I got here a little early. Take your time getting ready. Or go in scrubs. That works too," he said with a broad smile.

She started to smile, but her forehead became creased with distress.

"What is it?" he asked.

"There's a trauma with a pregnant woman coming in and Johnson asked me to stay, and . . ."

"It's okay. Do what you need to do. I understand," he said.

"Are you sure?" she asked, noticing the disappointment in his eyes.

"I get it. Go. I'll wait in case you're done in time for the show."

"If I'm not back, go without me." She paused and looked straight into his eyes. "I'm really sorry."

"Don't be. Do your thing."

She smiled sorrowfully and rushed out the door.

FOUR HOURS LATER, BETTY TRUDGED INTO the residents' lounge. Her eyes went wide when she saw the table set with candles and takeout containers, and Khalil waiting for her. She was so surprised, she just stood with her mouth hanging open, unable to speak.

"I thought you'd be hungry, so I ordered Vietnamese food and bribed everyone else to stay out of here for a while. I've been checking with the nurses' station to see when you'd be done."

"I figured you had gone to the show."

"Nah. What's the point?"

"But you wanted to see . . ."

"I wanted to see it with you. We'll catch another one. So, come on. You must be hungry," he said, pulling out her chair.

"Famished," she replied as she sat down. She found herself staring at Khalil as if she was truly seeing him for the first time and was overcome with a feeling of warmth. Looking into his eyes, she softly said, "Thank you for this."

He smiled. "Help yourself," he said, gesturing at the containers. "That's the insanely spicy curry you like."

Half an hour later, they were sitting side by side on the floor, leaning against the wall, their bellies full.

"Dinner was so good. Thank you again. I'm sorry about tonight."

"Don't be. This was perfect."

"I had brought a dress with me and everything," she said.

"You did?"

Betty nodded. "I wanted to look nice, since we're always in scrubs."

"You always look great to me. No one rocks scrubs better than you," Khalil said, gazing into her eyes.

For a moment she didn't look away, but then she caught herself and stammered, "Uh, the show, it's probably the second act by now. What do you suppose it was about anyway?"

"It's a musical, a love story. By now, the guy is professing his love to the girl. There's probably a big choreographed dance number. You know, like in real life."

She giggled. "I would have liked to see that."

"Well, let's recreate it ourselves," he said, taking her hand.

"Oh, I don't know . . . I . . ."

"Come on," he said, rising.

Betty stood up and Khalil put one hand on her shoulder and the other on the small of her back. They started to dance around the room. At one point, he said, "There's always a spin, you ready?"

She nodded and he spun her out, and back to him, a smile etched on her face. "One more before the finale," he said, and he twirled her out again and then held her in a grand dip. He slowly helped her rise, their faces only centimeters apart. Softly, he whispered, "I love you."

"Are we still acting out the show?" she asked, hardly able to exhale.

He shook his head and put his hand on her cheek, leaned forward, and pressed his mouth to hers. When their lips parted, he looked into her eyes with unadulterated adoration, cradled her face in both his hands, and they started kissing passionately. Eventually, she pulled back and tried to catch her breath.

"I think we got swept up in the moment," she mumbled.

Khalil took her hand and said, "I'm in love with you. I'm completely, head over heels in love with you. Every time you walk into the room, I can barely breathe."

"You never . . ."

"I never said anything because I was afraid of scaring you off. You're my best friend and I didn't want to risk losing you. There were times I almost said something, but you always stopped me, like maybe you knew and you weren't ready."

She dropped his hand and stepped back, muttering, "Maybe you're just feeling lonely, or . . ."

"Betty, I hate spicy food, but I always eat it with you." She looked at him with eyes like saucers and he continued, "You're the smartest person I know so part of me thinks you must know that, but you keep ordering even hotter dishes, not because you want to torture me but because you want me to like what you like, and you think I'll get used to it." Her eyebrows were sky-high. He stepped forward and stroked the side of her face. "I know you and I love everything about you—what a committed doctor you are, the way you look in these scrubs, your ponytail bouncing up and down when you're racing down the hallway, the look on your face when you have a really good Scrabble word, and the glint in your beautiful blue eyes when you see my mouth is on fire from the takeout we're sharing. Mostly I love the way you look at me when we're alone, because I can see it in your eyes, that you feel the same way." She just stared at him as if unsure of what to say or do. He pulled her close, caressed her cheek again, and swept her up into a frenzied kiss. They were kissing and running their hands through each other's hair when Betty pulled back.

"I . . . I . . ." she panted.

"Do you love me?" he asked.

"I don't believe in all of that."

"Betty, it's not something you believe in, it's something you feel."

"Feelings can mess everything up, make things harder, make us feel attached to things that aren't real. I've spent my whole adult life trying to escape fantasies and build something on solid ground. Something real. Medicine is real. We're doctors. That demands all our focus. There's no time for anything else. I've worked so hard, and you have too."

"I'm not asking you to give anything up or change," he assured her. "I want us to be partners. In so many ways, we already are." She lowered her gaze. "Tell me why you're so afraid to give in to your feelings."

"I . . . I just can't do this," she stuttered. "I'm sorry."

"Betty . . ."

"Please, I can't," she said, stepping back. "I don't know what to say. Will you please just go? I'll clean everything up. Please."

Khalil looked at her through a haze of disappointment, nodded, and walked out the door.

Betty just stood there, trying not to feel.

CHAPTER 13

Albert was gazing out the window as the trolley rolled through Brookline.

"What are you thinking about?" Ryan asked.

Albert looked straight into his eyes and said, "Labor Day weekend came so quickly, and . . ."

"Tell me."

"This has been the best summer of my life."

Ryan smiled. "You killed it in those animation classes. Now you've landed this amazing job. I mean, they're one of the best comics publishers in the business. It's so perfect for you."

Albert blushed. "Thanks. But that's not what I meant. Spending the summer with you has been . . ."

"For me too," Ryan said.

"I love hanging out with your friends. They're so cool. They always make me feel like I belong."

"You do. They're your friends too now, Al. Everyone loves you." Albert smiled and Ryan continued, "Speaking of which, Lucy broke up with another loser. So, no way to tell if she'll be off-the-charts happy or totally inconsolable tonight. Oh, and she said something about cooking, which is truly terrifying. Brace yourself."

AFTER BEING BUZZED INTO THE BUILDING, Albert and Ryan stood outside the locked apartment door.

"It's awfully quiet. You sure she's having people over?" Albert asked.

Ryan banged on the door again. "Luce, we're here! What's the password?"

The door flung open and Lucy shouted, "The password is *surprise*!"

Albert saw a big banner hanging on the wall totally askew that read, *Congratulations, Superboy!* Surprise and joy washed across his face.

"Surprise," Ryan whispered as Albert looked at their friends, all wearing glittery cardboard tiaras and holding colorful party blowers like at a child's birthday celebration.

Lucy ushered them into the apartment, placed a party hat on each of their heads, and the group started hooting their blowers.

Albert couldn't stop smiling. "What's this for?" he asked, wide-eyed.

"Your new job," Ryan explained.

"Now you're officially one of us," Lucy said, throwing her arms up dramatically. "Bottom rung. Underpaid. Starting out. Creative, artistic, desperate, and stupidly hopeful. Isn't it fucking great? Come on, get a drink and check out the buffet."

They said hello to their friends, grabbed a couple of wine coolers, and followed her over to the dining table, which had been pushed against the back wall to make room for a dance floor.

"Check it out," Lucy said excitedly.

"Wow, you made all this," Ryan said, perusing the table of casserole dishes each filled with a nondescript gooey substance.

"Uh-huh. I was slaving away. It was a great distraction after the fiasco with that asshole who shall not be named."

Al, I'll have to fill you in on my latest sad tale. Grab something to eat. I need a refill," she said, holding up her red plastic cup.

After Lucy flitted away, Ryan tried to pick up the plastic serving spoon stuck in one of the casserole dishes. He could hardly lift the spoon. "Uh, it's literally congealed. I'm truly afraid. Maybe we should stick to potato chips."

"I'll take a plate. It was so nice of her to do all this," Albert said.

Two hours later, Albert and Ryan were sitting close to each other on the couch while the others danced.

"I still can't believe you ate that wretched casserole concoction. You doing okay?" Ryan joked.

Albert nodded. "Tonight has been . . ." He stopped and shook his head. "Whose idea was it to throw this party for me?"

"Mine. Lucy was all in though as soon as I suggested it. I didn't know she'd want to cook."

Albert smiled. "This party is the nicest thing anyone's ever done for me. Thank you."

"You are so welcome." They stared at each other for an intimate moment and Ryan continued, "What you said on the train about it being the best summer. I meant it when I said me too. I care about you so much. So much."

"Me too. Ryan, do you want to spend the night at my place?"

"Yes," he whispered, and he leaned forward, touched Albert's cheek, and kissed him.

Albert pulled back mid-kiss.

"What's wrong?"

"It's just . . . not in front of everyone . . . I . . ."

Ryan stood up, ran his hand through his hair, and mumbled, "I can't fucking do this with you. I can't do this anymore."

"Wait, I—"

"No, I'm done," Ryan said, and he walked away.

Albert couldn't believe what was happening; suddenly, it was like everything was moving in slow motion. He had a ringing in his ears and could feel his heart beating out of his chest. He took a few deep breaths and got up to look for Ryan, walking through the kitchen and out to the small back porch where he came face-to-face with him.

Ryan grabbed a pack of cigarettes and a lighter off a little table, lit a cigarette, exhaled a line of smoke, and turned away. Albert came up behind him and touched his shoulder, but Ryan shrugged him off.

Albert took a step back. "I'm sorry. We agreed no—"

"No public affection, I know." Ryan turned around to face him. "Al, that was months ago and it was supposed to be temporary. With where our relationship is now, I can't believe it's still even an issue. My God, everyone in there knows we're together. They're our closest fucking friends."

"I know. It was just an instinct. I shouldn't have done that."

"You want to spend the night with me for the first time, but you won't even let me kiss you because you're terrified our friends might see and take a picture. Do you know how messed up that is? How that makes me feel?"

"I'm so sorry. I . . ."

"Please, don't try to justify it," Ryan said, dropping down into a chair. He put his head in his hands, took a long moment, and then looked at Albert. "You hurt me; do you get that? I like you so much, and I felt like we had become really close, but you still treat me like I'm a secret. Something to hide. Something to be ashamed of."

"I didn't mean it that way. It isn't about you; it's just how I've always been, because of how I grew up in this weird fishbowl."

"Maybe I can't relate to how you grew up or why you're so scared, but what I do know is how it makes me feel. I honestly thought you'd be past this by now, that the longer we were together, the more comfortable you'd feel just being yourself."

"I don't know what to say to fix this," Albert mumbled.

"Look, you've got some stuff to figure out. Until you do, we can't see each other. I just can't do it anymore. Not like this."

Albert felt like he couldn't breathe. His gaze dropped to his feet as he tried to compose his thoughts. "Please . . . I . . ."

"We can still try to be friends, eventually. I just need some space for a while."

Albert looked up and tried to steady himself. He saw the resolve in Ryan's eyes and murmured, "Yeah, okay. I understand. I'll go."

"That's not what I'm saying. You don't have to go. It's your party."

"They're your friends."

"Al, they're your friends too. This doesn't change that. I just need some space. We can keep our distance, or if you're too uncomfortable, I'll leave."

"No, it's okay. I should go." Albert started to walk away, turned back, and said, "Ryan, I'm really sorry. I didn't mean to mess everything up."

He shuffled through the apartment to the front door. Lucy saw him and ran over. "Al, are you leaving already?"

"Thank you so much for the party. It was incredibly sweet of you; it's just . . . I have to go," he muttered as tears began to fall from his eyes.

"Oh, honey," Lucy said, wrapping him in a hug.

He sniffled and pulled back. "I'm sorry. Thank you for everything."

By the time Albert made his way onto the street, tears were streaming down his cheeks. He used his sleeve to wipe his face and started toward the trolley station. With a lump in his throat and a stabbing pain in his stomach, he wondered how he could have managed to ruin the best night of his life.

CHAPTER 14

Soon it was the evening before the final day of the shoot. As they were finishing their meal, Michael said, "Jean, so this is it. Tomorrow is your last day of filming. That's pretty major."

"Eh," he replied, dismissively waving his hand.

"Come on," Michael pressed. "Someone like you retiring. It's a big deal. What are your plans? Any travel?"

"As always, I'll return to France to edit the film, put together the trailer. The film, she is not done, even after you all pack up and leave."

"Yeah, but after all that?" Michael asked.

"I do not think about after," Jean replied, taking a swig of his drink.

Michael laughed. "You may want to rethink the whole retirement thing. Really doesn't seem to suit you."

Jean shrugged.

Michael turned his attention to Georgia and Roo. "What about you two? Does what happens on set really stay on set, or do you have big plans?"

"Big plans indeed," Roo said. "We're planning to do a bit of a tour of Iceland and then figure out where we'll go next, but it will certainly be together."

"That's great. Seems you're following in Finn and Ella's footsteps. I'm happy for you both," Michael said.

Roo slung his arm around Georgia, kissed the side of her head, and said, "We're happy too."

Georgia gave him a little smile and then looked across the table at Jean and Michael and said, "Oh, speaking of my parents, I keep forgetting. My siblings and I are putting together a video for their thirtieth anniversary. Would you two please each record a short message for them and email it to me?"

"Sure thing," Michael replied. He huffed and said, "Jean, given how things began that summer, can you believe they've lasted decades?"

"Sometimes it takes a bump in the road to give one perspective," Jean replied.

"What do you mean?" Georgia asked, looking confused.

"Your parents fell deeply in love early on in our summer together, but your mother wasn't exactly ready for it. Back then, Ella . . ."

Jean was interrupted when Gunnar came into the room and said, "Excuse me. Mr. Mercier, the caterer is on the phone with some questions about the wrap party."

"Very well," Jean said, using the table for support as he slowly rose.

Once he was out of the room, Michael said, "That guy is in for a rude awakening. I can be pretty dense about things, but one thing is crystal clear, he's not ready for retirement. Films are his whole life."

"Yeah, but it must be taxing at his age. Perhaps he can find an artistic outlet that requires less intense commitment," Roo suggested.

"It's not just the filmmaking, it's the whole thing. It's this," Michael said, gesturing around the room. "He loves going on location, setting up camp, building a temporary family with the cast and crew. It's not just about the art, it's his way of life. It's who he is. People don't change."

Georgia's eyes drifted down to her lap as she thought about Michael's words. Roo noticed and whispered, "Darling, you look deep in thought."

She looked into his warm eyes. "I'm just a bit sleepy. Tomorrow's a big day. Let's turn in."

Georgia and Roo excused themselves. When Jean returned, Michael asked, "Everything okay?"

"There's always some damn aggravation when you're reliant on hiring locals. Every place, every film, every crew. I won't miss all the hassles," he grumbled as he retook his seat.

Michael chuckled. "Keep telling yourself that. For a guy who hates bullshit, you're really a pro, my nomadic friend."

THE NEXT MORNING, THE ACTORS WERE ALL feeling mixed emotions as they meandered from their trailers to the set. "Listen up!" Jean called as everyone huddled around. "As we always film out of sequence, I have never before shot the final scene of a film last. There is a first time for everything." He stopped to huff. "And a last time, I suppose. Today, we are filming the final scene of the shoot, of the film, and indeed, of my catalog." Some cast and crew became teary-eyed, putting their hands supportively on each other's backs. Jean stopped them, shaking his head and barking, "None of that shit. Don't forget, you still have a job to do. I'm not paying you to stand around fucking consoling each other like a group of coddled children."

"Oh, come on, Jean! Admit it, you're gonna miss us and all of this," Michael shouted.

Jean dismissively waved his hand. "I'll get enough of it and you when I'm editing the damn thing. But if you're so eager to memorialize the experience, wait until the wrap party. There will be plenty of booze, food, and a dance floor, though you won't see me on it."

Everyone laughed and Georgia hollered, "Never say never!"

Jean smirked. "Alright. Alright. Back to the scene. The old man is lying in bed, dying, his only two companions by his side. He and Georgia have their last words and she goes outside, overcome with emotion. Then he and Roo exchange their words, after which Roo goes outside to find Georgia, and we have our final moment. The camera will follow Roo from inside the house to outside in a continuous action. Places, everyone."

The cast got in position, Michael lying in bed tucked under the covers, Georgia sitting on the edge of the bed, and Roo standing.

"Rolling . . . Action!"

"Would you like a cool compress on your forehead?" she asked.

Michael slowly shook his head and tried to extend his shaky hand. She took hold of his hand, gently caressing his pale, paper-thin skin. His lips began to tremble, like he was trying to say something.

"You don't have to speak," she said.

He took a labored breath and murmured, "Thank you, Giselle, for bringing light into this house and looking after me so diligently. You have made the end bearable."

Her eyes began to fill with tears.

He squeezed her hand, let go, and said, "Please leave us. We have some final business to discuss."

She nodded as her eyes overflowed. She rose, leaned over, and kissed his forehead, before smiling at him one last time through her tears and exiting the room.

Michael struggled to lift his hand again, gesturing at Roo.

"It's okay," Roo said, taking his hand and sitting on the edge of the bed.

"The memoir. My legacy . . ." he muttered.

"Don't worry. It's done and I've followed your instructions to the letter."

Michael nodded ever so slightly. "Before you go, promise me . . ." He paused to take a breath as Roo leaned closer. "Promise you'll take care of her."

Roo looked at him quizzically. "The book or Giselle?"

"Yes," Michael replied.

"I promise."

A soft smile slid across Michael's face and he closed his eyes. Roo took a moment, rose, and walked through the small house and out the open door where he saw his lover, standing with her back to him, the spectacular landscape unfolding all around them. He came up behind her, slung his arms around her waist, and placed a tender kiss on the top of her head. She sniffled and put her hands on his forearms.

"I never imagined this would be so difficult," she said.

"Me neither. I also never imagined I'd meet someone like you. We can leave this place now. Together, if you wish."

They held each other for a moment, and she shuddered. "I can feel it. He's free." Tears trickled down her cheeks. She smiled and softly said, "Look what he's left us with. So much sadness. So much beauty."

"Cut!" Jean hollered.

Georgia wiped her face and Roo said, "That was brilliant. Are you okay, love? I could feel the authenticity of the emotion."

She nodded. "I guess I'm just a bit blue. Tapped into it. That scene was the beginning of the end."

"Only of the film, darling. Our adventure has only just begun," he said, kissing her forehead. "Come on, let's go get our notes."

CINEMATIC DESTINIES

AFTER HOURS OF FILMING, JEAN FINALLY YELLED, "Cut! That's a wrap!"

The cast and crew exploded with cheers.

"Before we pack up and head back to the inn for the party, I'd like to call each of the lead actors to take a bow," Jean said. "Rupert Reed!"

Roo trotted over to Jean and took a bow as everyone clapped, Georgia screeching at the top of her lungs as Roo's cheeks turned rosy.

"Georgia Sinclair Forrester!" Jean announced.

Georgia skipped over and joined Roo to more applause.

"The star of our film, Michael Hennesey!" Jean announced.

Michael joined his castmates to more cheers. He bowed and then said, "We all know the real star of this film is the legend, the icon, the artist himself: Jean Mercier!"

The cast and crew pounded their feet, clapping, hooting, and hollering.

"Jean, I know it's not your custom, but you have to join us in a final bow," Michael insisted, taking his hand.

Roo, Georgia, Michael, and Jean held hands and took a bow to thunderous applause. When they rose, Jean said, "Thank you all for this extraordinary experience. Now change into your street clothes and we shall celebrate at the inn." The crew began disassembling their equipment as Jean turned to the actors and said, "Such a fine group for my last hurrah. Thank you."

Georgia gave him a huge hug. He patted her arm and said, "I'll see you at the bar."

Roo took her hand and they started toward their trailers. "I can't believe it's over."

"Yeah, me either," she said forlornly.

He stopped, looked at her adoringly, and said, "Darling, remember it's just the film that's over. Our adventure is only beginning."

Georgia looked at him and took a breath as if she desperately wanted to say something but stopped herself. "It's just been an emotional day. I'll meet you after I change."

"Then we can dance the night away. Probably a good time to mention I have two left feet, which will no doubt be stomping all over yours," he said with a laugh, "so I wouldn't suggest wearing sandals."

She smiled and said, "You really are adorable."

"Just try to remember that when I'm embarrassing you on the dance floor."

"I'll see you in a few."

"Hurry, darling. I can't bear to be apart," Roo said, lifting her hand to his lips and kissing it.

TWO HOURS LATER, GEORGIA AND ROO WERE on the dance floor holding each other and swaying as if they were the only people in the room.

"You must be relieved it's finally a slow song. I'm not clobbering you quite as horrifically," Roo joked.

"You're a better dancer than you think," she said with a smile.

"Well, now I know you love me. I'm glad to see we're still in the honeymoon part of our relationship where our oddities come off as adorable and endearing. I imagine I'm in some trouble when the novelty of my ineptitude wears off."

She giggled softly and looked down.

"What is it, love? Have I frightened you? I can take dancing lessons if it's important to you."

She raised her gaze until their eyes met. "No, it's just . . ."

"What, darling?"

"What you said, about it being the honeymoon phase. Don't you ever wonder if maybe . . ."

"What? That reality will come crashing in and we'll bore of each other?"

She raised her eyebrows and nodded.

He laughed. "Of course not. I could never tire of you, and I promise to do my best to stay interesting and keep you on your toes. See, and I'm already off to a good start. You've been on your toes all night, fearing for your safety no doubt."

She smiled, took a moment, and timidly said, "Actors become infatuated with each other on set all the time. It rarely lasts."

"That's what makes it all the more special when it does. There's nothing to fear. This is much deeper than infatuation. I love you, now and always," he said in a more serious tone.

"I love you too," she said.

"How about we retire for the evening? It looks like things might wind down soon," Roo said. He then noticed Michael and a couple of crew members throwing back shots and jumping up and down as if they were in a mosh pit. "Ah, or perhaps it will keep raging all night. But we could still turn in and try to drown out the noise. We have so many plans to make. We can curl up in bed and figure out what's next."

Georgia glanced over at Jean, sitting alone at the table and nursing a drink. She looked back at Roo. "I'd like to spend a little time with Jean, see how he is. Can I meet you upstairs?"

"Sure," Roo said, pecking her lips. "I'll say a quick good night to Michael, if he'll even hear me. I hope he doesn't try to get me to do shots again. He's relentless. I'll meet you upstairs when we both break free."

Georgia traipsed over to Jean, affectionately squeezed his shoulders, and plopped down beside him. "Are you enjoying yourself?" she asked. "I hate to see you all alone. Are you sure you're not up for a little spin on the dance floor?"

"You're a dear to ask, *ma chérie*, but I have always preferred to observe, stay out of frame as we say."

She smiled. "Are you pleased with how the shoot went? We all felt like it was something very special."

"Indeed. Although between us, I hope I didn't become too sentimental."

"What do you mean?" she asked.

"The endings of my films are usually quite opaque, often dark. I don't like pretty packages tied neatly in bows. And I don't like to spoon-feed audiences as if they're too lazy or stupid to do the heavy lifting themselves, even if they are." Georgia giggled and he snickered and continued, "But with this one, perhaps sentimentality or senility got the better of me. I wanted to make my point clear."

"You did, without sacrificing any of the poetry. It's gorgeous. Besides, you didn't tie up everything. We don't know if the lovers choose to be together."

The glimmer of a smile flashed across Jean's face. He watched as Georgia glanced over at Roo, who looked like he was finally extricating himself from Michael and the others. Roo threw her a goofy smile and then winked before leaving the room. She turned back to Jean and said, "So tell me, it's your film, do you think they end up together?"

"I'm more interested in our real-life lovers." She raised her eyebrows and he continued, "You and Roo. It doesn't take much to see he's madly in love with you. From where I sit, it seems mutual."

She glanced down. "Yes, it's just . . ."

"Tell me, *ma chérie*. I'm a better listener than it may seem."

She took a breath, looked at him, and said, "Roo is the most incredible guy I've ever met. We have a deep connection and love each other very much. But it's not like I expected anything like this to happen. I wasn't looking for it. I've always been a wanderer. Now Roo wants us to plan a whole life and . . ."

"You're scared out of your fucking mind."

"Something like that."

"You are so much like your mother. I feel as if I'm speaking with her thirty years ago. It's remarkable."

"My mother?"

"Ella wasn't exactly ready for your father."

Georgia furrowed her brow. "You've insinuated that before, but what do you mean? They fell in love on location, got engaged, and got married, like out of a fairy tale. We couldn't be more different, me and my mother. Love is everything to her. She fell for my dad and never looked back."

Jean smirked. "It's true they fell in love that summer in Sweden. Your father wanted to marry her, couldn't wait to start their life together. Ella had never committed herself to a man before. Never even entertained the idea. She was terrified by what your father proposed, so she ended the relationship. Devastated him."

Georgia looked perplexed, but then warmth spread over her face. She smiled and patted Jean's hand compassionately. "Jean, I think you're confused because I look so much like my mother. It's okay. That could happen to anyone. I do love Roo, and I am scared, but I didn't say I'm going to leave him."

"Bloody hell, I'm not senile," Jean snorted.

"Oh, I know. It's okay if you're a bit confused. It's been a long day and it's . . ."

"For fuck's sake," he growled with exasperation. "I'm talking about your parents. I was there that summer. I had a front-row seat to their love affair." Georgia still looked confused, so Jean waved his arm around and called, "Michael! Come here."

Michael tottered over and slurred, "Hey, Jean. What's up?"

"Do you remember what happened between Ella and Finn at the end of our summer in Sweden?"

"Ella dumped Finn. Broke his heart. It was brutal."

Georgia's eyes were like saucers.

"Go back to your drinking and stupidity," Jean said to Michael.

When they were alone again, Georgia looked at Jean as if she could barely formulate words. Eventually she said, "My parents never told us that. They're such romantics. My siblings and I always thought . . ."

He touched her hand. "Ella and I had been dear friends for ten years before she met your father. Many men pursued her, as I'm sure many have pursued you." Georgia blushed and he continued, "She never showed real interest in any of them. She wasn't looking to settle down. Ella was always a free spirit, a traveler, full of passion and wanderlust. Your father threw a wrench into her life's philosophy."

"But they're together, so something must have happened."

"Love happened. Love, Georgia. Suppose she just surrendered to it. I wouldn't dare presume to speak for Ella, but from the looks of things over the last few decades, it seems to have worked out. Ask your mother about it sometime."

Georgia sat quietly for a moment, processing Jean's words. Eventually she muttered, "Thank you for sharing that with me and for listening. I should probably go upstairs. Roo is waiting for me."

"Of course, *ma chérie*."

She rose as if she was going to leave but then stopped herself and said, "Jean, can I ask you something?"

"*Oui*."

"Do you believe that romantic love is real, or do I sound ridiculous even asking that when we both know fairy tales don't exist and the princesses probably just wanted to get the hell out of the castle to see the world?"

He let out a puff. "What *you* believe is all that matters. But you do so remind me of your mother."

She gave him a peck on the cheek and slipped away.

GEORGIA OPENED THE DOOR TO FIND ROO sitting in bed, flipping through a tourism book, his phone in his lap, pillows stacked behind him. "There you are, darling. I've been skimming this little gem, and I think I've found a couple wonderful places to stop. How do you feel about a wellness buffet, which I think is code for vegetarian?" She furrowed her brow and he explained, "There's this charming little coastal town called Borgarnes. Looks perfect for a light scenic hike and lunch. According to online reviews, there's a fabulous restaurant in one of the oldest houses in town. On one side the wall is built into the rocks, and on the other there's a bit of a water view. Well, if you squint perhaps. Anyway, apparently the squash soup is a must."

Georgia tried to muster a smile, still hovering in the doorway.

"What is it? Pureed soup doesn't appeal?"

"No, it's not that. It's just . . ."

Roo tossed the book on his nightstand. He extended his arm and said, "Come here, love."

She kicked her shoes off and crawled into bed, burrowing into him.

He looked into her eyes and asked, "Is everything alright? You seem a bit far away."

"I'm okay. It's just . . ."

"The wellness buffet? I know, but I don't think they mean it in a pretentious Hollywood way. I think they're for real."

"It's not that." She paused for a moment and said, "Roo, what are we going to do after exploring Iceland? We've talked about being together and traveling, but how would it work? You live in London."

"I figured we'd have a home base somewhere. I'm not wedded to London. It could be wherever we choose. London, Los Angeles, Timbuktu. Hardly seems to matter as long as you're there."

She smiled faintly. "That's sweet."

"Although if you choose LA, be warned, we English never tan, we only burn. Fear not, I have a floppy sun hat of sorts, the kind a fisherman with no hope of catching fish might wear. Some have intimated it's a bit of an eyesore, but perhaps you'll find it fetching."

Georgia let out a soft giggle.

"Have I gone too far? You look truly afraid. I can ditch the hat and just stay indoors if that suits you better."

She ran her finger from his eyebrow down to his chin. "Roo, no one has ever made me feel this way. You are the funniest, sweetest, most oddly charming man I have ever met. I feel so close to you. Closer than I ever thought I could feel to someone. It's like you're my lover and my best friend all at once."

He planted a soft kiss on her lips. "I feel the same about you. You're so beautiful inside and out. I've never wanted anything more than how I long to be with you. Nothing has ever felt more right. For a long time, I was dreading the end of the film, but now I can't wait for tomorrow to begin our journey together, and all the tomorrows after that."

"What if there were no tomorrows?" she asked. "What if this moment is all we have?"

"Then I'd want to spend it making love with you," he whispered, and he began kissing her as they slowly undressed each other.

CINEMATIC DESTINIES

ROO WOKE UP THE NEXT MORNING, WIPED the sleep dust from the corners of his eyes, and noticed Georgia fully dressed sitting across the room in a chair. He stretched his arms and smiled at her, but it morphed into confusion. "Did I oversleep?"

She shook her head. "I woke up early."

He got out of bed, put his underwear and pants on, and sauntered over to her. "Just give me a minute to brush my teeth, love."

When he returned a few minutes later, she was sitting hunched over with her eyes glued to the floor.

"Darling, what is it?" he asked, kneeling in front of her.

She looked into his eyes, stroked the side of his face, and softly said, "Roo, I've decided to go back to LA. There's this place that does short-term rentals, mostly for actors. I stayed there a while back, and I left some of my stuff in their storage room. I emailed them this morning and there's an apartment I can have right away."

"I don't understand. I thought we were going to explore Iceland a bit more before settling on a home base. Have you landed a job or something? I'm happy to go to LA, it's just a bit of a surprise."

"No, I didn't get a job, and I wasn't suggesting you come with me. I . . ."

He furrowed his brow. "What are you saying?"

"I think I should go to LA and you should go back to London. Or if you want to see more of Iceland, then . . ."

"Georgia, what on earth are you talking about? I wanted to see Iceland with you. I wanted to see everything with you. We were planning a future together."

"Roo, I told you I'm not good at relationships. I tried to warn you, but . . ."

"The past doesn't matter. Only what we do now. This is *our* relationship, no one else's. We can make it as we wish. I have complete faith in what we share together."

"I can't do it," Georgia said. "I'm sorry. Truly, I'm so sorry. I love you. More than I ever thought I could, but I want my life to be an adventure. I'm not ready to give that up."

"No one's asking you to. We can have an adventure together," he said, profound hurt in his voice.

"Roo, I want to be an actor going from project to project, and I want to travel wherever I'm inspired to go. That's not how relationships work. You'll grow tired of it, and you'll resent me, or I'll resent you."

"Darling, don't you know I love you for exactly who you are? I don't want to change you or hold you back. I believe we can blossom together. Please, if you'll just take a chance on us, on love."

She took a deep breath and said, "I'm sorry. I'm so sorry."

He looked at her like he couldn't believe what he was hearing, rose, and walked to the door. "Georgia, I know you don't believe that people belong to each other, but you're wrong. Deep down, you know it. That's why you cry at the end of *Breakfast at Tiffany's*. If you'd only take the risk, you'd see: love isn't a tether, it's a set of wings. I won't beg you. It has to be something we both want."

With that he left the room, quietly shutting the door behind him. Georgia sat perfectly still, trying to breathe.

An hour later, after Gunnar brought her bags downstairs, she went to the dining room to say her goodbyes.

Jean and Michael were sitting at the table finishing breakfast.

"Georgia, join us," Michael said. "But don't talk too loud. My head is throbbing."

She tried to muster a smile and replied, "I can't. They called a car to take me to the airport and it's here. I just came to say goodbye and thank you both for an extraordinary summer."

Jean looked at her with disappointment in his eyes. "You are leaving on your own?"

She nodded. "I need to go back to California for a while."

"What did I miss?" Michael asked, looking bewildered.

Before Georgia could respond, Roo came into the room. They exchanged an awkward look, avoiding each other's eyes, and Roo stammered, "Uh, fellas, I'm going to hit the road. Thank you for everything. It was . . ."—he stumbled as if unable to find the right word, glancing at Georgia—"it was unforgettable."

Jean nodded and said to Roo, "Please send my regards to your mother."

"Safe travels," Michael added.

Roo turned to Georgia and said, "Well, I guess this is it."

"Yeah, I guess so," she mumbled.

"Well, goodbye then," he said, and he pecked her cheek, a look of heartbreak on his face.

As soon as he left the room, Georgia turned to Jean and said, "Thank you for everything. I hope you're not disappointed."

He huffed. "I hope it is you who is not disappointed."

Michael jumped up and gave her a big hug. "Tell your folks I said hi. Thanks for a great summer. You're a pistol. Tell Ella she's got nothing on you."

Georgia smiled dimly. She approached Jean, leaned down, and wrapped her arms around him. "You're a beautiful artist, and I'm honored to have been a part of this film. Thank you for everything."

"The pleasure was all mine, *ma chérie*."

With that she left. As soon as she was out of the room, Michael looked at Jean and said, "What the hell was that?"

"History repeating."

AFTER A LONG TRAVEL DAY, THE BUILDING manager let Georgia into her small apartment.

"As you can see, it's pretty much like the last place you had. I had someone bring your boxes up from storage."

"Thank you," she said, taking the key. She turned to her driver. "You can just leave the bags there."

Both men left. She locked the door behind them, looked around at the cheap furniture in the dark space, and leaned against the wall to collect her bearings. No one knew she was back in LA, and she wasn't ready to tell anyone. As she stood there, images of Roo flooded her mind. She could almost feel the warmth of his embrace and suddenly felt the pang of a deep loneliness she had never experienced before. Too lethargic to make her bed or even search her cardboard boxes for bedding, she pulled her wool shawl out of her carry-on luggage, wrapped it around herself, and curled up on the couch. The faint smell of Roo was both haunting and comforting. Before tossing her phone on the coffee table, she decided to scroll through her messages. There were three emails from Roo; the first was a long message professing his love and asking her to take a chance on their future, the second was informing her he'd returned to London and giving her his address and phone number, and the final email was the last photograph taken of them inside the Blue Lagoon, him kissing her cheek as she beamed. The message simply said, *I love you*. When Georgia saw how happy she looked in Roo's arms, she burst into tears. Eventually, she cried herself to sleep.

CHAPTER 15

The next morning, Georgia awoke with puffy eyes and a lump in her chest. She dragged herself to the bathroom, brushed her teeth, and changed into workout clothes, convinced that a good run would clear her mind and shift her mood. After walking to the canyons near her temporary home, she did some stretches and started running. Her mind flooded with memories of Roo—and the many hikes they had taken together—and she began to imagine him running by her side, wearing the goofy hat she could picture so well although she had never seen it. "Snap out of it," she muttered, pounding the ground, trying to outpace the images reeling in her mind.

She returned to her apartment dripping with sweat, guzzled some water, and showered. Freshly dressed in yoga pants and a T-shirt, she looked around, unsure of what to do with herself. Noticing her unmade bed, she decided it would feel too lonely by herself. She curled up on the couch and turned on the television. As she flipped through stations, she noticed a *Monty Python* movie and burst into tears. The waterfall rushed from her eyes as her body heaved and she grabbed her chest, unable to lessen the pain. "I miss him so much," she sputtered through her sobs. "So much."

Georgia spent the next week running in the mornings, ordering takeout, watching television, sobbing her eyes out, and sleeping on the couch. Her depression only worsened. When she wasn't thinking about Roo, Michael's words started playing on a loop in her mind, "Ella dumped Finn," followed by Jean's words, "Your father threw a wrench into her life's philosophy." Even though she knew it must be true, she couldn't get her head around it. Feeling heartbroken and alone, she decided to go see her mother.

ELLA WAS IN THE YARD PICKING BLUEBERRIES when Georgia appeared out of nowhere, tapping her shoulder. "Mom."

"Oh, goodness. You startled me," she gasped. She caught her breath and looked at Georgia with concern. "What are you doing here? Is everything alright?"

"Yeah, everything's fine. I got back to LA a few days ago. Sorry, I should have called, but . . ."

"Nonsense," Ella said, sounding relieved. She put the bowl of berries down and hugged her daughter. "You're always welcome. What a nice surprise. Tell me, how was the film shoot? Did you get on well with Jean?"

"Yeah. I can see why you're such good friends. He's amazing. Irreverent and so artistic. It's kind of sad that was his last film."

"Hmm. Indeed," Ella muttered.

"Is Dad here?" Georgia asked.

"He has a voiceover job. He won't be back for a few hours." She looked at her daughter, took her hand, and said, "Sweetheart, if something's wrong and you need him, I'll call the studio. I'm sure he'll come right home."

"No, honestly, I'm okay. Actually, I came to see you. I was hoping we could hang out. Talk."

Ella smiled. "Let's take those into the kitchen," she

said, gesturing at the bowl of blueberries, "and I can make us some tea."

Georgia nodded and grabbed the bowl.

When they got to the kitchen, Ella turned on the tea kettle. "You can just leave those on the counter. Probably the last batch of the season. We were lucky this year to still get berries in September. Those beautiful bushes have always been generous. I'm going to make a tart for your father."

Georgia plopped onto a barstool and asked, "Why do you love those blueberry bushes so much?"

"You know that your dad had them planted as a gift for our tenth anniversary."

"Yeah, but it's such a weird gift. Like, he's a big movie star. He couldn't afford jewelry?"

Ella laughed. "I suppose it may seem strange if you don't know the story. Our dear friend Albie, the actor who . . ."

"Who costarred with Dad in *Celebration*. The one Albert is named after."

"Yes," Ella replied. The tea kettle whistled, and she stopped to fill their cups.

"Go on," Georgia encouraged.

"Albie was a special man. Your father and I were very fond of him. He was a crusty old bird in some ways, but he was also such a dear soul. He was a romantic who believed in love above all else. Lived by that belief. Taught us to do the same. When we were all in Sweden and they were filming *Celebration*, and I was freeloading off Jean for the summer, we celebrated what turned out to be Albie's last birthday. We didn't know about his cancer recurrence at the time, but later he confided in me."

Georgia looked at her mother intensely, hanging on every word.

"Anyway, that night Albie told us the story of how he met his wife Margaret, the love of his life. It was at a party in London. A blue-blooded, upper-crust soiree, which was definitely not Albie's scene. Margaret ended up there by chance, with no idea what kind of party it was, so she showed up in a casual dress with a homemade blueberry pie. Albie was hit by lightning the moment he laid eyes on her. Eventually, he saw her at the dessert table and sidled over to her. He took a piece of the pie she'd made and they started talking. He fell hopelessly in love with her on the spot. Ever since your dad and I heard the story, blueberries make us think of love. Grand, epic love." She crinkled her nose and shook her head. "I know it's silly, but they've become special to us. Our wedding cake was layered with blueberry preserves, to honor Albie who had already passed. Since then, for special occasions we've always found a way to have blueberries. And it's why your father gave me those bushes for our tenth anniversary, and why they're so special to me." Ella took a sip of her tea, a soft smile in her eyes.

Georgia looked down.

"What is it? Is something wrong?" Ella asked.

Georgia raised her gaze and asked, "Why didn't you ever tell us that you and Dad broke up?'

Ella furrowed her brow.

"Jean said that when filming wrapped on *Celebration*, you split up. He said you left Dad."

Ella sighed. "Yes, that's true."

"I don't understand. We all thought you fell in love on the set of the film and then Dad proposed to you at the premiere in Cannes."

"That's all true, but it's not the whole story." Ella stopped to take a breath. "Your father and I fell madly in love that summer. Neither of us had expected it, nor had we ever experienced anything like it before. At the time I was living in a little flat in Paris, but really, I had spent years roaming from one place to the next, no roots, no responsibilities. Your dad was in LA, living in this very house." She smiled and continued, "He wanted to get married. He asked me to move here so we could be together. He even offered to live in Paris or anywhere else I wanted. Anything so we could be together. But I was absolutely terrified of the way I felt for him. Love was new to me. I didn't know how to trust it. To trust it wouldn't abandon me or turn me into someone I didn't recognize."

"So, what happened?"

"I made the biggest mistake of my life. I told your father to go back home and get on with his life. He begged me, but..."

Georgia reached out and put her hand over Ella's.

"The moment he walked out the door of that inn was the most gut-wrenching of my life. I melted into a puddle of tears. I had broken my own heart, and his. But I didn't understand why I had done that, and I didn't have a clue how to fix it."

"What did you do?"

"I flew back to my place in Paris. Wept like a baby. I visited your grandmother in Spain. Cried on her shoulder. I got a therapist and did work on myself." She stopped to giggle. "I even got a kitten, so I could see if I was capable of taking care of someone else."

"Our cat growing up?" Georgia asked.

Ella nodded.

"That's why she was named Sweden. You named her after the place where you and Dad fell in love. As a reminder."

"Yes."

"When did you and Dad..."

"We didn't see each other again until the film's premiere at the Cannes Film Festival. We were standing on the center of the carpet, hardly able to exhale, and I told him everything that was in my heart. Begged for his forgiveness and for another chance. That's when he got down on one knee and proposed with a ring he'd bought after we left each other in Sweden. It turns out he had enough faith for the both of us."

Georgia's eyes became misty. "People always said he proposed at the premiere because you met when he was making the film. That you both wanted the whole world to know."

Ella smiled. "We know what people think. The truth was, it was our first chance to get engaged and we just couldn't wait. We didn't even notice anyone else was there. Our eyes only saw each other."

"Why didn't you ever tell us?"

"I've always been embarrassed. It was such a stupid mistake. And your father is a gentleman. Besides, we never saw any need. We committed ourselves fully to each other that day and never looked back."

Georgia sniffled.

"What is it, sweet girl? You can tell me," Ella said.

Georgia exploded in tears. "I fell in love, Mom. This summer. I've never felt anything like it in my life. Didn't even know it was possible to feel so much for someone. Without him it's like my insides have been torn out. It hurts so much. He's the greatest guy in the world and I screwed it up. Got scared and fucked it all up."

"Oh, sweetheart," Ella said, throwing her arms around her. She rubbed Georgia's hair and said, "It will be okay. You can try to make it right."

Georgia pulled back and wiped her face. "I don't know if I can. If he'll give me another chance. I don't even know if that's what I want. Maybe I don't believe in all of that. The thought of someone tying me down and trying to change me. Maybe it was just a love affair and I need to let it go. To really be free."

"Shh..." Ella whispered, caressing her daughter's hand. "I understand that wild spirit all too well. It's magical, and don't ever let anyone try to tame it. But if you find someone strong, who loves you for exactly who you are, with whom you can be more of yourself, not less, that's a very special thing."

Georgia sniffled and said, "I didn't think anyone would get it, least of all you. I was wrong. You do understand. Thank you for being here for me."

Ella smiled. "Be happy, sweet girl. Whatever that means for you. Take some time. See how you feel in your heart of hearts. Trust yourself. Then you'll know what to do."

"COME HERE," FINN SAID AS HE AND ELLA slipped into bed. He extended his arm and she crawled into the crook, her cheek on his chest as he wrapped his arms around her. "Seeing Georgia was a nice treat. She was awfully quiet, though. That's so unlike her. When dinner was over, she fled as fast as she could. Didn't even stay for that delicious tart you made."

Ella looked up into his eyes and said, "She's going through a tough time. She's in love."

Finn started to smile, but it turned into confusion. "I don't understand."

"She came by this afternoon to speak with me. Apparently, she fell madly in love this summer. Thinks he could be the one."

"That's great. Isn't it?"

Ella sighed as her gaze fell. "She got scared. Fucked it up. Now she doesn't know how to make it right, or even if she's ready to try." Finn rubbed her shoulder. She looked back up into his eyes and said, "Turns out you've been right all these years. She's just like me. If you ever use that against me..."

"I won't," he whispered, dropping a kiss in her hair.

"She knows that we broke up at the end of our first summer together. Jean told her. I guess the kids always thought what the rest of the world thought, that we fell in love on set and that's why you proposed in Cannes. Minus the messy bits." She sighed and lamented, "We should have dispelled that illusion a long time ago. I'm afraid that one grand red-carpet moment has cast a big shadow that the kids have lived under."

"Even if that's true, where there's a shadow, there's light." She looked at him curiously and he explained, "The kids have seen how we live. The truth of our feelings for each other will outshine any shadow the media or public fantasy has created."

She squeezed him tighter. "When Georgia asked why we never told them about our breakup, I felt bad, as if we had lied to them somehow."

"We didn't. We've been together longer than any of them have been alive. There was never any reason to tell them."

"Finn, the reason would have been so they'd know that love can be complicated and messy. People make mistakes, screw things up. Things don't always go perfectly, but that doesn't diminish the love, or that it's worth fighting for."

"I guess I don't really see it as messy or complicated," he said. "Not with us. The truth is, I don't regret a thing. I'm glad things happened the way they did."

She raised her eyebrows. "How can you say that? Don't you remember what it was like?"

"Sweetheart, losing you was the most painful thing I've ever gone through. Even when I look back now and think about the other tough times in my life—the issues we've had with the kids over the years, losing my parents—none of it was unbearable because we had each other. Leaving Sweden without you, those agonizing months that followed . . ." He stopped to shake his head. "It was torture. The worst part was that as much as I was hurting, I knew you were in just as much pain and I couldn't help you." He lifted her hand to his lips and kissed it. "But it was all worth it. You needed that time to be sure about us the way I was. When we got back together, you were ready. Thirty blissful years later, I've never looked back."

"Me either."

"It all happened the way it was meant to, baby."

Ella smiled. "From the moment we got back together, I knew it was forever. Do you remember how magical our honeymoon was?"

"Every minute of it. God, the Amalfi Coast is spectacular."

"And that sublime house you rented us on the water with the views of those incredible rock formations."

"You would run around topless on our private beach, so carefree. And we made love over and over again. On the beach, by the infinity pool, standing outside against the exterior of the house because we couldn't make it to the bedroom," he said, running his fingertips down her arm.

"I had never felt freer. It's funny," she said, crinkling her nose and shaking her head. "I was afraid that love, commitment, marriage would somehow make me less free, but it was just the opposite. There was one moment on that trip that . . ."

"What, baby?"

"Do you remember the day we went into town? We wandered around the shops and bought those beautiful hand-painted serving dishes and table linens, so we could entertain at home and bring our friends a taste of the Amalfi Coast." He nodded and she continued, "We strolled around the old town eating gelato. Then you had arranged dinner at the chef's table at that amazing little hole-in-the-wall.

When the chef learned I was interested in cooking, he gave me a lesson."

"I had so much fun watching you," Finn said. "Flour across your forehead, trying to understand what he was saying through his thick accent. You were so into it."

"And then we stumbled onto that little outdoor bar with that wonderful band. We danced under a canopy of stars. Do you remember?"

"You were wearing a short turquoise sundress, cinched at the waist, with a ruffle on each shoulder."

She looked at him in surprise.

"I told you, I remember every minute," he said.

"When we got back to the house, we undressed each other. You pulled me onto your lap, brushed my hair back, and we began making love. We looked deeply into each other's eyes. It was so profoundly intimate, and that's the moment I knew."

"What, love?"

"The closeness between us was as certain as the sunrise. When we decided to share our lives, I was ready to take the leap. In that moment, I knew it wasn't a leap at all." He smiled and she added, "From then on, anything was possible. If I were to fall, you'd catch me. And I'd catch you. We could each be ourselves, forever. Boundless. I felt entirely content, serene."

"Me too," he said, kissing her softly. "I knew something had changed. The next day, on the beach."

"You did?"

He nodded. "I have a confession, more than thirty years in the making." She looked at him curiously and he said, "It may be ridiculous, but men want to make a certain impression when they're wooing a woman. Like we've got game. With you, I couldn't even pretend to be smooth." Ella blushed. He pecked her lips and continued, "The first night we spent together in Sweden, it wasn't about sex. I wanted you to feel about me the way I felt about you. I had fallen so deeply for you. I thought if we made love, you would see it, feel it, and maybe you'd allow yourself to love me that way too. And you did, but I always sensed there was some part of you that couldn't fully give into it. Something you held back." She started to lower her gaze, but he skimmed her cheek, and she looked straight into his eyes. "On our honeymoon, the day after we went into town, I was relaxing on a lounge chair, and you were running around on the beach, splashing in the water with abandon. You looked back at me, giggling, and I could see it in your eyes. To my core I knew that you had finally allowed yourself to love me as much as I love you."

She kissed him softly. "Thank you for marrying me. For waiting until I was ready."

"Thank you for marrying me."

They shared a quiet, intimate moment before Ella said, "Finn, do you think Georgia will be okay?"

"Yes. If it takes her some pain to get to the good stuff, in the end, it will be worth it."

"I think she really loves this guy. You should have seen her eyes when she spoke of him. I've never seen her like that before."

"That reminds me of something your mother once said. The night I met her, she told me how you'd gone to visit her in Valencia after our breakup. She said you were a wreck and that she'd never seen you like that before."

Ella huffed. "Today with Georgia, it was almost like looking in a mirror at myself thirty-one years ago."

He dropped another kiss in her hair. "If he's really the one, it will work out."

"How do you know?"

"I believe in love."

She smiled. "Me too."

CHAPTER 16

The next morning while Ella was having tea, she decided to FaceTime Jean.

"*Ma chérie.* What a wonderful surprise. I've been thinking about you."

"Oh?"

"Georgia was sublime in the film. I enjoyed getting to know her. Reminds me so much of you, in every way. A rare beauty, a firecracker with a warm soul. Wait until you see her performance. Somehow she inherited your spirit and Finn's talent."

Ella smiled. "It meant a lot to her, and to all of us, that you cast her. It's extraordinarily special and full circle for our family, and especially me. Thank you."

He came as close as he ever did to a genuine smile. "The honor was all mine."

"Seems you told her some of my secrets."

"You know I only tell people what they must hear. Comes from spending a lifetime as an artist. Plus, I'm too damn old to filter," he said with a snicker.

"What was your excuse before?" Ella joked. "I'm just needling you. Truly, I'm grateful for *all* you've done for Georgia."

Jean nodded almost imperceptibly. "It's always a pleasure to see your beautiful face, but I can tell when you have an ulterior motive. I can still read your eyes, even through my own sagging lids."

"Yes, do you look like death warmed up," she teased.

He laughed. "I was possessed by an idea last night, for a film. Usually when that happens, I get up and bang away on a script until I can sleep. With no more scripts, there's nowhere to put the ideas, so the bloody things keep spinning in my head. There's no respite."

"Funny you should say that. It's exactly why I'm calling. Rumor has it, you're retiring. But you know I never believe gossip. Especially when it seems so utterly absurd."

"Sometimes the rumors are true, vicious as they may be."

"You're an artist. Artists make art."

He smiled softly and let out a puff. "I'm tired, Ella."

"You'll have plenty of time to sleep when you're dead, which from the looks of it isn't far off." The corners of his mouth curled upward, and she continued, "Albie knew he was dying the summer he came to film *Celebration*. For fuck's sake, unlike you, he had cancer. That didn't stop him. Quite the contrary. It motivated him to make a final piece of art that would live on long after he was gone. Seems like a better use of time than waiting around to die."

Jean smiled, squeezed his eyelids shut for a long moment, and then looked directly at Ella. "You know I don't believe in looking back. Sentimentality, nostalgia, longing, pining over one's own legacy—all rubbish. Tragic misuses of imagination. Pathetic human foibles. Flaws of our bleak condition."

"No need to sugarcoat it. Tell me what you really think," she joked.

He chuckled. "I do find myself looking back, Ella."

"And?"

"I've fucked some things up for sure, especially with the fairer sex. Perhaps I missed out on something. But I've had a bloody good run too. Made a hell of a lot of films. Some of them are even good." Ella smiled. Jean's expression became softer, and with a wistful look in his eyes he said, "With all I've done, I find myself most often thinking about that summer in Sweden, making *Celebration*."

"I think of it often too."

"*Celebration* was about the meaning of life. The inevitable tragedy of the human condition. The trivial nature of our existence. Yet I do believe it was on that set, during that magical summer, I began to see a glimmer of something else—a glimmer of hope."

"And they say you can't teach an old dog new tricks."

"Promise you'll never tell anyone. Even after I'm gone."

"Your secret is safe with me."

"You know, Ella, you're the love of my life, platonic as the relationship may be."

"No. Filmmaking is your great love. Always has been. But I do love you too, as much as one can love a morbid, narcissistic, and royally fucked-up genius."

He laughed. "I do so love you. And your gorgeous family."

"And we love you." A quiet moment passed and she added, "Will you please think about what I said?"

"I shall think of nothing else."

"I'll see you at the film's premiere, if not sooner. Our whole family will be there to support Georgia, and you. Be well, my dear friend."

"You too. Thank you, *ma chérie*. Thank you."

AFTER ANOTHER SLEEPLESS NIGHT, ALBERT tried to make progress on his new work assignment but was too consumed with thoughts of Ryan. He decided to FaceTime Georgia.

She had just stumbled into her apartment after a long run, her face flushed and dripping with sweat. When she saw it was her brother, she answered, panting. "Hey, snot face."

"Are you okay?" he asked.

"Just got in from a run," she sputtered. "Give me a second." She guzzled a bottle of water and caught her breath. "I'm here. What's up?"

"It's about a guy."

Georgia smiled. "Go on."

"I've been seeing this guy, Ryan."

"Is he hot? Did you fuck him?" she asked, raising an eyebrow.

Albert sighed. "It's not like that. We were taking it slow, and I really like him; it's just . . ."

"What's wrong?" She softened her voice and said, "You can talk to me."

"He broke up with me because I'm not open . . . especially with Dad."

Georgia looked at him compassionately and said, "Sweetie, why don't you just tell Dad? It's not a big deal and he won't care."

"How do you know that?"

"Because Dad's not a dick."

"But what if—"

"I know you're worried about it, but you don't need to be. There's no reason to twist yourself into knots. Let me get Betty in on this call. She'll tell you the same thing."

"Georgia, I'm not sure if she knows. I don't—"

"Sorry, too late," Georgia interrupted.

"Well, hey you two," Betty said, wearing her blue scrubs. "I'm having the longest shift ever. You caught me on a break. I'm in the residents' lounge about to eat a PowerBar from the vending machine. It's not even the flavor I like. Yes, my life is sad." When neither Georgia nor Albert reacted, she said, "Oh my God, is something wrong?"

"No, nothing's wrong. Not really. It's just . . ." Albert stammered.

Georgia jumped in. "Al's gay. The guy he likes dumped him because he's not out with Dad. Mom knows, but he's afraid to tell Dad."

"Georgia!" Albert wailed.

"Oh, Albert," Betty said softly, a warm smile on her face. "Thank you for telling me."

"That's not exactly what happened," he muttered.

"I don't want to pressure you, but I really don't think there's any reason to be worried about telling Dad. I mean, he's the greatest ever. I know we all feel that way," Betty said. She looked at Albert tenderly through the screen and continued, "Look objectively at how he lives his life. He always treats everyone with respect. He and Mom have a diverse group of friends, many of whom are gay. Plus, he cares deeply about social justice and has great politics."

"Yeah, that's exactly what I said. He's not a dick," Georgia said with exasperation.

A smile flickered across Albert's face.

"Al, you're completely awesome exactly as you are. Mom and Dad love you like crazy. Live your life. Be who you are full force," Georgia said.

"I couldn't agree more," Betty added.

Albert smiled. "Thanks. As annoying as you two can be, and even though I'll never forgive you for treating me like your doll when I was little, I got pretty lucky in the sister department."

"Damn straight!" Betty exclaimed.

"We are amazing," Georgia joked. "Seriously Al, just be you."

"I'm trying," he replied.

"Okay, so now that we've settled that, let's get back to the good stuff. Tell us about the guy. Is he sexy?" Georgia asked.

Albert blushed.

"Ooh, it seems he is!" Georgia squealed.

"Can I ask you two something for real?" Albert said. They nodded and he continued, "I don't have that much experience with guys. But with Ryan . . ."

"Yeah," Betty gently encouraged.

"The way he makes me feel. Sometimes I think it's everything. When we're together"—he stopped to shake his head—"it's just the best feeling. Like I'm more alive with him than I could ever be without him. Everything feels possible. I'm not just who I am. I'm who I want to be." Betty and Georgia looked at him wistfully, as if they understood deeply. Albert continued, "Why is it so hard to let go of everything else and just grab onto it?"

Betty sighed and softly said, "I don't know."

Georgia looked down and inhaled deeply. In a barely audible voice, she whispered, "Me either."

"Yeah, that's what I was afraid of," Albert said.

CHAPTER 17

Georgia was curled up on the couch under a blanket, the shades drawn in her drab apartment. She grabbed her laptop off the coffee table and switched it on, resolved to delete Roo's last message. Before she could complete the task, her inbox beeped. There was a new message from Jean with the subject line "Anniversary video." She opened it and read it aloud. "*Ma chérie*, forgive that I have not made a personal message for your parents. I have always preferred to remain behind the camera, so I sent something else in its stead. When making a film, I have the camera operators record some of what happens on and around set, behind the scenes. I went through my archives from *Celebration* and edited together this video of your parents the summer they met—stolen moments when they had no idea that a camera was capturing them. Raw, naked footage of two people falling in love. Pure beauty. I thought your family would enjoy seeing it. Between us, I must confess it was watching your parents that magical summer, and all the years since, that made me believe all is not lost in the world and indeed love is real. Perhaps it will even make you believe. Love, Jean."

She opened the attachment and hit play. Suddenly, her parents, younger than she had ever known them, appeared on screen, her father strikingly handsome and her mother extraordinarily beautiful. Georgia gasped at the sight of them. Finn was tenderly stroking Ella's cheek, off in the corner of the set. The camera pulled closer as Ella looked down bashfully, and Finn gently kissed her forehead, washed in a look of unbridled new love. The corners of Georgia's mouth trembled as she leaned closer, the light from the screen forming a halo around her face. There were intimate snippets of her parents walking on the lawn, stealing a kiss outside Finn's trailer. They were radiant, full of hope, and unabashedly taken with each other, all when they thought no one was looking.

Georgia sat utterly mesmerized, a smile crawling across her face and her eyes flooding. Tears silently streamed down her cheeks as she watched the last moment, the cast of *Celebration* taking their final bow and Finn racing to Ella, picking her up, and twirling her in the air as she laughed, before they kissed passionately. "That must have been right before she left him," she muttered. "God, they look so impossibly happy." When the video ended, she grabbed a tissue and cleaned herself up. Then she forwarded the email to Betty and Albert, following up with a text message that read: *Just sent you a video of Mom and Dad. Watch it now.* She took a deep, centering breath and rose, finally knowing what she had to do.

KHALIL CAME INTO THE RESIDENTS' LOUNGE looking for Betty. "Hey, I brought you this," he said, handing her a PowerBar from the vending machine. "They restocked. It's your favorite kind."

"Thanks," she said, taking the snack but unable to meet his eyes.

He touched her hand and said, "Please, can we talk? It's been strange for weeks, since that night. You're my best friend. I don't want it to be like this between us and . . ."

She started to raise her gaze to meet his, but they were interrupted when her pager went off. "Sorry," she mumbled, pulling it out of her pocket. "Fuck," she said, tossing him the PowerBar.

"What's wrong?"

"Kate O'Connor needs an emergency C-section," she replied as she raced out the door.

Nearly an hour later, Betty shuffled into the residents' lounge, her head hung. Khalil was waiting for her. He sprang up from the bench and asked, "How'd it go?"

Betty shook her head almost imperceptibly, her eyes fixed to the floor. "She had a massive placental abruption. There was so much blood. I've . . ."

"Oh, Betty," he said, putting his hands on her shoulders.

"We saved the baby. But Kate . . . there was nothing we could do. There was nothing I could do. I—"

"You did everything you could," he assured her. "I'm so sorry. I'm so sorry." He pulled her close in a comforting embrace, rubbing her back.

For a moment, she leaned into it. Then she looked up into his eyes and said, "It was so awful. Kate was hysterical, begging us to save her baby. I'll never forget the look on her face as all her dreams evaporated." She paused. "This must have been my fault. If I had only caught it earlier, then . . ."

"No, Betty. Don't do that to yourself. She had excellent care. You were on top of her pregnancy from day one. Sometimes these things just happen, and it isn't anyone's fault. There weren't any warning signs."

"Maybe I got too attached to her, liked her too much, lost my focus," she said.

"That's not true. Caring about your patients makes you a better doctor."

"I don't know. I don't know anything," she mumbled, visibly holding back tears.

"You've got to let it out. Feel this. It's the only way through it," he said, stroking her cheek. "Let it out."

"I can't," she insisted, taking a deep breath. "I can't allow myself to feel it."

"Betty. You already do," he whispered.

She pulled back. "I'll be fine." She walked over to her locker and took out her belongings, placing her street clothes, bag, and cell phone on the bench. "I'm just gonna go home and take a hot bath and try to forget today ever happened."

Khalil walked over to her and gently said, "Look at me." She turned to face him, and he wrapped his arms around her. "Please, you've got to let it out. It's okay. It's okay to feel."

"I can't," she said, and shook her head as she began to tear up.

"Shhh, it's okay," he said, caressing her hair.

She burst into tears.

"That's it," he whispered. "Just feel it."

Betty sobbed uncontrollably, crying and heaving against his chest as she tried to breathe. He held her as the tears continued to flow through a stream of howls that sounded like a wounded animal, her body violently shaking. After what felt like an eternity, she pulled back, grabbed the tissue box off the table, and wiped her face. "I'm sorry for crying on your shoulder."

"Betty, I love you. God, I love you."

"Damn it, Khalil, don't you see?" she shrieked. "There are no fucking happy endings! Love hurts! It's filled with pain! People have nothing to gain and everything to lose."

"You don't really believe that. Naturally, you're upset. I'm here for you. Always. Lean on me and—"

"Please just go. I want to be alone."

"But . . ."

She turned her back to him. "Go. Please."

He sighed and said, "If you change your mind, let me know." He left the room, closing the door behind him.

Betty collapsed onto a chair, her knees in her lap and her head in her hands. After a few minutes passed, she sniffled and looked up, trying to muster the strength to go home. She noticed a message light flashing on her cell phone and read Georgia's text. She wiped her bloodshot eyes and opened the video, hitting play. "Oh my God," she mumbled as her parents appeared on screen. There was something so profoundly innocent and beautiful about the way they looked at each other, as if their souls were connecting off in the shadows, when they thought no one was looking. She burst into tears again, unable to control the waterfall gushing from her eyes, and for the first time, not wanting to. She cried and cried. As she watched the images of her parents, a film reel played in her mind with images of Khalil—his pained expressions when he ate spicy food, his silly victory dance when he won a game of Scrabble, the intensity in his dark eyes when he studied, the sympathy on his face when he spoke with his patients, and his broad smile every time Betty walked into a room.

"It's him. You're so stupid. It's always been him," she muttered. Suddenly, she jumped up and raced to the door, but it flung open before she could reach for the handle, and Khalil stepped inside.

"I came back to make sure you were alright. It kills me to see you so torn up," he said, looking at her wet, blotchy face. "Don't be mad. I just want to know if you're okay."

"I love you," she said through her tears. "I'm in love with you."

His eyes went wide as a huge smiled danced across his face. He put his hand on her cheek, gently wiping away her tears.

"I don't know if I'll ever believe in happy endings, but I believe in happy beginnings," Betty said. "Is that enough?"

"It's everything," Khalil whispered. He cupped her face in his hands and they kissed.

ALBERT DROPPED HIS KEY AND WAS PICKING it up when Ryan and his friends came barreling out of their apartment.

"Hey, Al," Ryan said.

"Hey," Albert replied softly, averting his gaze.

"We're just heading out to play laser tag," Ryan said.

"Oh. Well, have fun," Albert replied with a lump in his throat.

"Listen, Al, you can come with us if you want."

"Thanks, but I'm gonna stay in and try to do some work tonight."

"Are you sure? You're welcome to join us."

"That's okay."

"Well, see ya," Ryan said as he and his friends bounded down the hallway.

"Yeah, see ya," Albert mumbled.

Albert shuffled into his apartment, grabbed a can of soda from the refrigerator, and cracked it open. Soda in hand, he plopped down at the table and turned on his laptop, intending to immerse himself in his work project. He noticed new emails in his inbox and decided to scroll through them, immediately opening the message from Georgia and clicking on the video attachment. Suddenly, his parents flooded the screen, young and in love. It was so overwhelmingly beautiful that he smiled brightly as he watched, the glow from the screen shining on his face. "I always thought it was brave that you proposed in front of the whole world," he mumbled to the image of his father. "This is brave. Just letting yourself be so honest with someone."

When the video ended, he took a slow, considered breath and bolted out of his apartment, racing down the stairs and down the sidewalk straight into the heart of Harvard Square. He saw Ryan outside the bustling Harvard train station, people all around. "Ryan!" he shouted.

Ryan stopped and turned.

Albert tried to catch his breath as he continued to race toward Ryan.

"Al, did you decide to come with us?" Ryan asked.

Albert looked all around at the swarms of people, and then he looked directly into Ryan's eyes. "I came to do this," he said, and he put his hand on Ryan's cheek and kissed him passionately. Onlookers started cheering at the joyful scene, and a nearby street performer began playing a love song on his saxophone. Albert finally pulled back, and the onlookers went on about their business.

Ryan smiled. "I can't believe you did that."

"I'm sorry it took me so long. I wasn't ready before, but I am now. Is it too late?"

"Kiss me again," Ryan said.

Albert smiled and kissed him gently, but with no less passion.

"So, you're coming with us?" Ryan said.

Albert nodded and took his hand, and together they headed into the train station.

THE CAR PULLED OVER AND GEORGIA paid the driver.

"Miss, it's pissing down. Wait and I'll come around with a brolly."

"That's okay," Georgia said, quickly exiting. She threw her handbag over her head, raced up the stairs of the brownstone, and started searching for the right apartment buzzer, rain pounding down. She frantically pressed the button, holding it down over and over again, until she was buzzed inside. She flew up the stairs, leaving a water trail behind her. When she arrived on the third-floor landing, Roo was standing at the door wearing his terry cloth bathrobe.

"Georgia, what on earth?" he asked, wide-eyed. "Uh, come in," he said, reaching out his hand. She followed him inside. Completely dumbstruck, he stared at her and eventually stuttered, "Uh, you're sopping wet. Shall I get you a towel?"

She shook her head. "I don't care about that. I flew from LA because I had to see you. I didn't even have the patience to wait for the driver to open an umbrella."

The corners of Roo's mouth turned upward, and his cheeks became rosy. "Why did you have to see me?"

"Because I'm in love with you, positively, hopelessly, madly in love with you. I still want to make life a grand adventure, but not without you. Oh, Roo, I know I hurt you and I hope you can find it in your heart to forgive me. If you do, I promise to spend the rest of my life making it up to you."

"The rest of your life?" he muttered.

"If you'll have me."

"Wait. This isn't right."

Georgia's face fell. "Oh, I'm sorry. I hoped—"

"No, you misunderstand, my darling," Roo said with a soft smile. "Don't move an inch." He walked over to a nearby credenza, opened the top drawer, and returned holding a small black velvet box. "I just meant that I imagined how this would go. Shortly after I got back from the shoot, I stopped by my mother's flat and asked her for my grandmother's engagement ring. I knew you'd show up at my door or I'd show up at yours."

"You did?" she asked, tears in her eyes.

He nodded and caressed her cheek. "And I knew when the moment presented itself, I'd want to do this," he said, getting down on bended knee. He opened the jewelry box to reveal an oval-shaped ruby surrounded by diamonds. "Georgia Sinclair Forrester, you are the love of my life. Do me the honor of becoming my wife, and together we shall soar. Will you marry me?"

"Yes. Yes, I'll marry you," she said, salt water streaming down her face.

He slipped the ring on her finger and said, "The stone looks like fire, just like that burning spirit in you I so love." He rose, wove his hands into her curls, and they kissed. "Now come on, love. Let's get you out of these wet clothes."

CHAPTER 18

The day before the children were due to arrive home, Albert called Ella.

"Well, hello, my sweet boy."

"Hi, Mom."

"This is a nice surprise. My phone has been ringing all morning. Your sisters both called to say they're each bringing a friend for the weekend."

"Actually, that's why I'm calling. Can my friend Ryan fly back to California with me? He has relatives in LA."

"Of course, sweetheart. You'll have the jet to yourselves. The others are flying commercial because of scheduling issues. They won't be here until later in the day."

Albert was silent for a moment and then said, "He's my boyfriend, Mom."

Ella smiled. "That's wonderful. I didn't know you were seeing someone. Is it new?"

"Not exactly, it's just that Dad doesn't know. I . . . I'm planning to tell him tomorrow. Depending how it goes, I thought maybe I could invite Ryan to the celebration the following day."

"I would love that. Sweetheart, there's nothing to be anxious about with your father. There never has been. He loves you more than anything."

"I just . . ."

"What has you so worried?"

"I just don't want him to be disappointed."

"In you?" Ella said. "Not possible. He'll be glad you confided in him. I'm sure he'll also be thrilled to hear there's someone you care about. There's nothing to fear. Not a thing. I promise you."

Albert inhaled. "Thanks, Mom. I better go. I need to pack."

"See you tomorrow. I love you."

"I love you."

THE NEXT AFTERNOON, ELLA WAS STANDING at the kitchen sink drying dishes. Finn came into the room, slipped his hands around her waist, and whispered, "Hi, sweetheart," before kissing her cheek.

She took a slow breath and turned to face him. She leaned her forehead against his for a long intimate moment and then pulled back and stared intensely into his eyes.

"What is it, love?" he asked, stroking her cheek.

"Albert needs to speak with you. He's in his room."

Finn looked at her quizzically.

"When you're done, ask him to come down to set the outdoor dining table and you can help me with the grill."

"Okay, love," he said, walking off.

FINN LIGHTLY KNOCKED ON Albert's door.

"Come in."

Albert was lying in bed, but he sat up straight as a board when his father walked in.

"Mom said you wanted to see me."

"Yeah," Albert said softly, his shoulders clenched and unable to make eye contact.

Finn sat down on the edge of the bed. Albert inhaled deeply and then looked directly into his eyes. With a slight tremble in his voice, he said, "There's something I need to tell you."

Sensing his son's trepidation, Finn replied, "Whatever it is, you can tell me. I promise it will be okay."

Albert took another deep breath and said, "I'm gay."

A huge grin spread across Finn's face.

Dumbfounded, Albert asked, "You heard me, right?"

"Yes," Finn replied. "I'm just so relieved. With the buildup I thought it was something bad." Suddenly, Albert felt as if a spring had been released, and his shoulders relaxed, the tension leaving his body. Finn took his hand. "Thank you for telling me. You know this doesn't change anything. I love you exactly as you are. I always have and I always will."

Albert's eyes flooded.

"Oh, come here," Finn said, embracing him in a comforting hug. He whispered, "I love you, son."

Albert sniffled and softly said, "I love you too." He pulled back and wiped his face. "It really doesn't make a difference to you?"

"Only that I want to know who you are. It makes a difference that you told me. But it doesn't make a difference in any other way. Why would it?"

"I don't know. I . . ." Albert muttered.

Finn smiled. "Your mother and I have always only wanted you to be yourself. We have a simple hope for you and your sisters. To find something and someone to love."

Albert wiped his eyes again.

"So, is there someone special?" Finn asked.

"Yeah."

"Well, tell me about him."

"His name is Ryan. He's the reason I finally told you. We had some problems because I hadn't been open. That wasn't cool with him, and he didn't want to see me anymore. Not like that."

"I can understand that. When you care about someone, you want to be free to shout it from the rooftops if you feel compelled to."

"Yeah."

"How'd you two meet? What's he like?" Finn asked.

Albert smiled bashfully and said, "We met at school. He was a graphic design major, and we took a class together last semester senior year. He's so cool, really nice and smart. Because of him, there are all these fun things I do now and amazing people I've met. He's bolder than me, which I think is a good thing. When we're together, I have more fun than I ever do without him. We connect and feel close in a way I've never had with someone before."

"Do you love him?"

"It's been hard to find out until now. I like him. I like him a lot."

Finn smiled. "Then lean into it. There's nothing better than finding that person who makes your heart take flight. When you're ready, your mother and I would like to meet him."

"Actually, he's in LA. He flew down with me, and he's staying at his aunt and uncle's place in Los Feliz. I thought maybe I would invite him to come tomorrow . . ."—he ran his hand through his hair before continuing—"as my date. But tomorrow is about you and Mom so if that's not okay, it's totally—"

"We would love to meet him. He's more than welcome. Please invite him."

Albert smiled. "Thank you. For everything."

Finn patted his arm and said, "Your mother wanted help setting the outdoor table. Shall we?"

Albert nodded and they stood up. Finn put his arm around him and kissed the side of his head. He then playfully tousled his hair, and they headed downstairs.

Ella was placing a stack of dishes on the counter when they bounded into the room. She smiled brightly at the sight of their joyful faces. "There are my guys."

Finn walked over and kissed her cheek, and they stole a loving glance.

"Can you please bring that out and turn the grill on?" she asked, gesturing at the platter of meat and skewered vegetables.

"Sure," Finn replied, picking up the tray and heading outside.

Once he was gone, Ella turned to her son. "Well?"

He sprinted to her side and enveloped her in his arms. "Dad was totally fine with it. He said it doesn't change anything, and I could tell he meant it."

"I told you, my sweet boy," she said, rubbing his back. "He loves you more than he could ever say. Just like I do."

"He even said I can ask Ryan to come tomorrow. If it's okay with you."

"Of course it is," she replied, giving him a big squeeze before letting go. She looked at his smiling face and saw a lightness in his blue eyes she had never seen before. Her own eyes became misty, and she sniffled.

"Are you okay, Mom?"

"I'm perfect," she replied, wiping her eyes. "Now do me a favor and set the outdoor table. Betty texted and she and Khalil should be here soon."

"Sure thing," he said, grabbing the stack of plates and silverware and heading outside with a newfound bounce in his step.

Ella meandered outside and over to Finn, who was standing by the grill. She took him in her arms, held him close, and whispered, "Thank you for being you. I love you."

"I love you too," he said, pulling back and gazing into her eyes. "You had to know it wouldn't make a difference to me. Please tell me you knew that."

"Of course I did. It was Albert who was anxious. I told him there was no need, that it wouldn't matter."

Finn looked down and said, "I feel terrible. I must have done something wrong for him to be so worried about telling me. For him to think it could change things in the slightest. I guess I screwed up."

Ella touched his cheek. "Look at me." He raised his gaze and she continued, "You're a magnificent father. You didn't do anything wrong. It was just hard for him. Maybe it's difficult between fathers and sons sometimes."

"When did he tell you?"

"When he was seventeen. But he didn't really tell me. He came home crying one day, and I was trying to comfort him. I made it clear that I already knew, and that it didn't matter and had never mattered. I love him as he is. That's when he opened up. I told him there was no reason not to tell you, but he wasn't ready. I hope you understand that it wasn't my place to reveal something so personal. It had to come from him."

"I know," he said, lifting her hand to his lips and kissing it.

"I didn't give you a head's up today because I knew it wasn't necessary. I trusted you completely. I knew how you'd react." Finn smiled and she continued, "He never dated. Didn't you ever suspect?"

"It's crossed my mind over the years, but he's always been shy and a late bloomer, so I never really knew." He huffed. "I realize now that you've known since he was born.

Do you remember when he was only two days old, and we were in bed with him? He was falling asleep in your arms after you nursed him. Do you remember what you said? The promise you asked me to make?"

Ella smiled softly. "I remember. I told you that I loved him with all my heart and asked you to promise to always do the same."

"I had no idea why you were saying that, but the look in your eyes was so intense, so heartfelt. I said of course I'll always love him and asked what you meant. I'll never forget your reply." He paused and shook his head. "You said, 'Finn, you have to love him the way you love our girls. You can't treat him any differently because he's a boy. If he falls down and gets hurt, you need to hold him and be tender. Be gentle with him, always. Never break his heart or his spirit. Promise me, Finn.' You were so earnest that all I could say was, 'Yes. I promise.' I never knew why you said that until today. How did you know?"

"They're my babies. I know them," she whispered, tears in her eyes. He gently wiped the wetness and she said, "I didn't know anything specific, but when I looked into his innocent eyes, in the deepest part of my soul I felt that he might need some extra love and support from us, that's all."

He kissed her forehead and said, "The best thing I ever did was to fall in love with you and make our beautiful family."

"I feel the same way," she said, pressing her mouth to his.

The moment was broken when Albert hollered, "Guys, stop making out. Betty and Khalil are here!"

Ella and Finn giggled and sauntered over.

"Oh, my angel," Ella said, wrapping Betty in an embrace.

"My turn," Finn said, giving his daughter a big hug.

"Hi, Khalil," Ella said. "It's so nice to see you."

"Yes, great to see you," Finn added, shaking his hand.

"Thank you for having me. I'm honored to be included in such a special occasion," Khalil replied, slinging his arm around Betty.

Finn and Ella exchanged a curious glance and then looked at Betty's serene expression.

Ella said, "Uh, if you two would like to unpack, we set up the blue guest room for Khalil, but perhaps . . ."

"Thanks, but that won't be necessary. Khalil can stay with me in my room." Betty turned to Khalil, and they smiled at each other. She turned back to her parents and said, "We're much more than friends. We're in love."

"I love your daughter very much," Khalil gushed, before pecking Betty's cheek.

Ella and Finn beamed.

"It's terrific, sweetheart," Finn said.

"How wonderful! We couldn't be happier for you," Ella added, surprise on her face.

"What is it, Mom?" Betty asked.

"To be honest, I didn't know if you believed in romantic love. I'm so glad that you do."

"I'm not sure I believe in happy endings, but Khalil and I both believe in happy beginnings. That's all we need." They smiled at each other, and Betty turned back to the group. "I never knew you could fall hopelessly in love with your best friend. The only downside is that Georgia turned out to be right."

"No surprise there!" Georgia screeched as she flitted out back, holding a young man's hand.

"Little peach!" Finn exclaimed.

"Hi, Dad," she said as they hugged.

Georgia proceeded to greet the others.

When she hugged Albert, he whispered in her ear, "I told Dad. He was fine with it, and my boyfriend is coming tomorrow."

"That's great, snot face," she whispered affectionately.

"You're on time," Ella remarked. "I'm speechless."

Georgia laughed. "You can thank my better half for that. Everyone, this is Roo." Before anyone could greet him, Georgia continued, "My fiancé."

"Oh my God!" Ella squealed.

"As always, a hell of an entrance," Betty joked.

"Your fiancé?" Finn asked in disbelief.

"We fell madly in love over the summer," Georgia said, looking into her beloved's eyes.

"Yes, we did," Roo added, kissing Georgia's forehead. He turned to Finn and said, "I hope you're not traditional and that you'll forgive I didn't ask for your blessing. I just couldn't wait a single moment to ask this beauty to spend the rest of our lives together. You see, I can't possibly live without her."

"Nor I without you," Georgia said as they stared into each other's eyes.

"I can relate," Finn said. "The same thing happened when I met Ella. When you find the one, everything changes."

"Thank you. My mum said she can't wait to talk to you both. She thinks it's some kind of poetic fate that Georgia and I met doing a film with Jean. She remembers fondly her summer filming *Celebration* when you two fell in love," Roo said.

"So do we," Finn replied, draping his arm around Ella.

"Well, there's a whole lot to celebrate. How about I fetch us some champagne?" Ella suggested.

The kids all nodded.

Finn followed her into the kitchen to help. Ella began fixing a serving tray with snacks—cheese, crackers, olives, nuts, dried figs and apricots—while Finn popped two bottles of champagne and started filling flutes.

Georgia vaulted into the room and flitted over to Ella. She squeezed her shoulders and said, "I wanted to say thank you, for our talk when I came over."

"I'm so happy for you," Ella replied.

"Look at my ring," Georgia said, holding her hand up. "It was his grandmother's. The stone reminds him of me."

Ella smiled. "It's absolutely beautiful. He must love you very much. You didn't tell me it was Rupert. Heavens, I remember when he was just a wish in his mother's heart. Then when she was pregnant, and later when he was born."

"Me too," Finn added, filling the last glass. He chuckled. "It's funny because Charlotte and I played spouses in *Celebration*, and in real life, we all felt like family on that set. Now we are family."

"And so it continues, life imitates art," Ella remarked. She huffed and mused, "Or perhaps art inspires life."

Just then, all the others ambled into the kitchen.

"We came to see if you needed help, or lost your way," Betty said.

Finn smiled and said, "Everyone, pick up a glass. We can toast and then bring everything outside." When each person had a glass raised, he slung his arm around Ella and continued, "To Georgia and Roo. We wish you a lifetime of happiness. Love each other fearlessly and you will live in a constant state of hope. That's our wish for all our children. To love. Cheers."

"Cheers!"

Everyone sipped their champagne. Finn and Ella put their glasses down and looked deeply into each other's eyes, as if discovering a whole world no one else could see. They smiled softly. Finn planted a tiny kiss on the tip of her nose and rested his forehead against hers, stealing an intimate moment.

The others all found themselves staring.

Khalil whispered to Betty, "Your parents are very much in love."

"They sure are," she replied.

"It's great, isn't it?" Georgia whispered.

"The best," Albert agreed.

CHAPTER 19

Ella opened her eyes and turned to see Finn sitting beside her, propped up against pillows. She slung her arm across his stomach and whispered, "Good morning, my love."

"Good morning, sweetheart," he said, sweeping his fingers down her arm until they found her hand.

"I heard you tossing and turning last night. How long have you been awake?"

He sighed. "A while. I just can't get Albert off my mind. He started crying, Ella. When I told him I love him and that nothing had changed, he burst into tears. Like he had been so afraid of how I would react. It gutted me."

"That's because of how deeply you love him," she said, giving his hand a supportive squeeze.

"Clearly, I messed up. Failed him. I—"

"No more of that," she interjected. "Look at me." He looked into her eyes, and she said, "You're his Superman. Don't you see that? He admires you more than anyone. He's still finding his footing. It must have been incredibly daunting to tell you of all people something that feels so big to him. It's not because of anything you did wrong. It's because of his sensitive, extraordinary soul, how much he adores you, and the bond you two share."

Finn lifted her hand to his lips and kissed it. "Thank you."

"I'm only telling you the truth."

"I hope that's how he feels."

"He's so happy his boyfriend is coming today," Ella said. "That's because he wants to introduce you two."

"I'm looking forward to meeting him. Albert told me a little about him. They sound like a good match, like they balance each other."

"Oh, Finn, I'm so glad the kids each have someone special. Don't get me wrong. They're all still so young and it's not like I'm trying to marry them off, or that I care if they ever choose to marry. It's just that I want them to know what it's like to love with an open heart. The joy, giddiness, lust, comfort, exhilaration, even the devastation. All of it. I want them to know what that is . . . what it is when we let go of our borders. I want them to experience that beautiful space where the trees touch the sky and we can no longer tell what's what, and we don't care."

"Me too."

"Now come here and snuggle me. It's our wedding day after all."

He laughed, scooched down beside her, and they lay face-to-face. He caressed her cheek and whispered, "God, I love you."

"Good, because I love you." They shared a quiet moment and Ella said, "We're going to have to drag ourselves out of bed. Brunch is in a couple hours. The caterers dropped everything off last night, but there's still a lot to do, heating things up and setting the outdoor table."

"How are we dressing for today?" he asked.

"Casual for brunch. Then I thought you and I could change before the ceremony. Maybe it's silly, but I bought a wedding dress."

Finn kissed the tip of her nose. "My bride, even more beautiful today than the day we met."

"Thank goodness your eyesight has declined."

He laughed and tenderly ran his finger from her brow to her cheekbone. "Trust me, I see you exactly as you are."

"No, you see me as *you* are, through the filter of those generous, loving eyes. That's the magic of what love does."

"It sure is."

"Finn, today let's celebrate that despite the challenges life brings, we somehow always manage to love each other."

"Show me," he said with a devilish look as he slipped his hand under her nightgown. "Let's start the day off right."

"We have to set up the table."

"It can wait," he said, weaving his fingers into her hair and kissing her passionately.

"OH MY GOD, MY FACE HURTS," ELLA SAID as everyone continued to laugh hysterically.

"It's true," Roo insisted. "Jean almost had a bloody stroke."

"I can picture the whole thing," Ella sputtered through her laughter.

"Well, this has been so much fun, getting to know everyone," Finn said, looking around the table at his children each seated beside their special guest. "Would anyone like more? I think I should get those leftovers inside."

"I'll help," Ryan offered, rising. Albert grazed his hand, and they exchanged smiles before Ryan grabbed a quiche and followed Finn into the kitchen.

Finn put plastic wrap over the leftovers and loaded them into the refrigerator. "Thank you," he said to Ryan.

"I know today is a family event. Thank you for having me," Ryan said.

"It's our pleasure," Finn replied. He took a breath and continued, "I actually wanted to apologize for not having met you sooner. Albert told me that caused some problems in your relationship, and I'm so sorry." He stopped and shook his head. "Ella and I always wanted our family to feel close. We wanted our kids to feel loved and supported for who they are. Clearly, I did something wrong as a father to make him so anxious about being open with me. That was never my intention and I feel awful. I was up half the night trying to figure it out and—"

"Sir, you didn't do anything wrong," Ryan interrupted. "Al loves you guys more than anything in the world. He feels super close to all of you. It's the reason I wanted to meet you so badly. Because of how important you are to him. Being a part of this family is everything to him."

Finn ran his hand through his hair. "Really?"

Ryan nodded. "You're all so accomplished, confident, and larger than life. Al's quieter. That's just his way. He worries that means maybe he doesn't fit in as much, but I think it's what makes him fit in even more. It makes him special."

"I think so too," Finn said.

"He always goes on and on that his mother is the sweetest person in the world, his sisters are the smartest and most talented, and you, well, Al completely worships you. You're his hero." Surprise and joy washed across Finn's face. Ryan continued, "You're the reason he took those animation classes over the summer. He thought if he could use his artistic skills to do something in filmmaking, it would be another way to be close to you. To have something in common and be more like you, but in his own way."

"I . . . I don't know what to say," Finn stuttered. "I just assumed that I had screwed up and . . ."

"It's just hard for some guys to tell their fathers, that's all. In Al's case, it's because of how much he loves you. Looks up to you."

Finn smiled warmly. "Thank you. Thank you for telling me all of that. It means a lot to me."

"You're welcome. I probably shouldn't have pressured him. I just wanted our relationship to be free, for him to be free. Truthfully, with how he gushed about you guys I also wanted to see what all the fuss was about. Now I get it."

Finn chuckled. "Sometimes we all need a little push. It's nice to see how well you know him and that you care about each other."

"We do, sir. I do," Ryan said, straightening his shoulders.

Finn patted his back. "Shall we rejoin the others?"

When they got outside, Ella said, "I think we should all go change. Let's meet out back when we're ready."

Soon Finn was waiting outside in a simple black suit, underneath a canopy of wildflowers created for the day as a nod to Ella's wedding bouquet thirty years earlier. The kids each stood beside their partner. Ella appeared in a strapless sea-colored gown with a tea-length tulle skirt, her long spirals partially pulled back and adorned with small crystals. Finn could hardly exhale when he saw her. Their eyes glued to each other, she walked to her beloved, and they stood face-to-face, holding hands.

"You are stunning. You take my breath away," Finn said.

"I picked the dress because it's the color of your eyes."

He smiled bashfully. "Shall I go first?"

She nodded.

"Ella, I fell in love with you so quickly, so deeply. I never thought it would be possible to love you more than I already did. Yet my love has grown and deepened with each passing day. When I look at you today, I see the gorgeous, sexy, brilliant woman I met all those years ago, but I see so much more: the excitement on your face every time we explored a new travel destination, the look of love in your eyes each time you told me we were expecting, the wonder in your eyes when we saw sonogram images and heard the heartbeats of our children, the tenderness on your face when you cradled our babies in your arms, the anticipation in your eyes as you watched them take their first steps. I see your face during countless moments—your joy, courage, compassion, worry, heartache, and enthusiasm. I see all the laughter, happiness, and closeness during every private moment we have shared. Ella, my partner, my one true love, today I take you for who you have been, who you are, and who you'll become, and for all that we've created together. Thank you for all the moments. I will spend every remaining moment of my life loving you. I choose you. I choose us. Always."

Tears filled Ella's eyes. Finn used his fingers to brush away the salty water.

"Oh, Finn, when you were talking, all that I could think was that during all those moments, what I saw was the look in *your* eyes. We've shared so much." She caressed his cheek and he smiled. "When we first met, I was terrified of my feelings for you. I loved you so deeply. It was all new to me. I didn't even understand what that kind of love was. When I tried to compare it to other things, tried to make sense of it, I was always left feeling more adrift. That's because love isn't like anything else. Love isn't about me, or you. It's about this intangible thing we create together. Love exists in the space between where we end and another begins. Thanks to you, my whole life has happened in that glorious space." He smiled and she ran her finger across his eyebrow. "Finn, we made the decision to keep our relationship at the center of our lives, no matter anyone or anything else. That has been our great secret and why I can look around with such pride at all we've created and then look back into your eyes and know that it was always the two of us. I promise to love you for all my days. I choose you. I choose us. Always."

Finn took his bride's face in both his hands, and they kissed passionately.

Everyone began clapping. Betty, Georgia, and Albert all found themselves overcome with emotion, sniffling and dabbing their eyes. Betty smiled as tears trickled down her face. Khalil used his thumbs to gently wipe the wetness. When Betty composed herself, she announced, "We have a gift for you. Let's all head to the screening room."

The group moseyed to their home theater. Betty, Georgia, and Albert stood in the front of the room, while everyone else settled into leather recliners.

"Mom, Dad, we love you both so much," Betty began. "You're the best parents anyone could hope for. Thank you for supporting us and allowing us each to become who we are."

"Because we turned out fabulous," Georgia chimed in.

Everyone laughed and Betty continued, "We feel so grateful to have two such special people as our greatest role models, and to see the strength you two have together. You've shown us what it means to love. Thank you for the example you've set."

Finn draped his arm around Ella, and they exchanged a tender glance before turning their attention back to their children.

"I got this," Albert whispered to Betty with newfound confidence. He looked at his parents and said, "We're so happy to be here celebrating your anniversary with you. We knew many others would also want to share their best wishes. Betty had the great idea of reaching out to your friends and asking them to make video messages. We edited them together as our gift to you."

Ella beamed. "How incredibly sweet. I can't wait to see this. Thank you."

"What a wonderful gift. Thank you," Finn added.

"Jean refused to be on camera," Georgia said with an eye roll, "so he put together something even better, which is at the end of the video. We hope you love seeing it as much as we did. Happy anniversary."

"Happy anniversary," Betty and Albert said.

Albert ran to shut off the lights and turn on the video, and the kids all took their seats.

Finn and Ella smiled, laughed, and shed a few tears as they watched the videos sent by their friends scattered around the globe, espousing messages of the joy felt watching their love story, and their hope for many more chapters. The cast of *Celebration* came last—Willow Barnes, sitting in her Broadway dressing room, Charlotte Reed in her London flat, and Michael Hennesey by his pool in the Hollywood Hills—each remarking on the extraordinary summer they all spent together that changed all their lives. And then suddenly images of Finn and Ella from thirty-one years ago were on the screen.

Ella gasped and her eyes instantly flooded.

"Oh my God," Finn muttered.

"Jean said he always records behind-the-scenes footage on his shoots. He went through his archive for *Celebration* and edited this together for you," Georgia explained.

Ella smiled, tears cascading down her face. Finn held her close, rubbing her shoulder as they sat watching, surrounded by their children, all bathed in the glow of the screen. Near the end, the cast of the film took their final bow. "Oh, dear sweet Albie," Ella whispered through her tears. "He'd be so happy to see us now." Finn pecked her cheek, and they watched the final moment as Finn picked her up, spun her around, and they kissed as if no one were there. Albert paused the video, with a frozen frame of the last image. Ella and Finn looked at each other with wet cheeks and smiling eyes.

"I've spent my life making films, but that," Finn said, stopping to shake his head. "I don't even have the words. I would never have expected Jean to be so sentimental, so romantic at heart. Age has been good to him."

"And to us," Ella murmured. "That was so beautiful."

"You are so beautiful." He wiped the tears on her face and whispered, "I love you with all my heart. I always have and I always will."

"And I love you with all my heart."

They kissed softly and rested their foreheads together, lost in a whirl of memories, hopes, and serenity in the moment.

Ella pulled back, looked around the room at their family, and then at the image on the screen of her and Finn gazing at each other with unbridled love, with the cast and crew of *Celebration* in the background. She turned back to Finn, stroked his cheek, and whispered, "Thank you for doing this with me."

"Doing what, my love?"

"Life."

EPILOGUE

May 2   *Entertainment News Report*

It seemed all of Hollywood was out last night for the premiere of *Beauty*, slated to be legend Jean Mercier's final film. The night was full of surprises. Flexing their star power and showing their gratitude to the now ninety-year-old filmmaker, it was a veritable who's who on the red carpet.

Willow Barnes stunned in a strapless Versace gown. The former fallen tween star revived her career when Mercier cast her in his acclaimed film *Celebration*, for which Barnes won the Oscar for her supporting role. Once the most followed person on social media, the reclusive actress hasn't walked a red carpet in over a decade, although she remains a presence on the silver screen and Broadway stage. When asked why she decided to make a rare public appearance, the blonde beauty explained, "Jean changed my life. There is nowhere else I would be."

Barnes wasn't alone. With the exception of deceased actor Albie Hughes, the entire cast of *Celebration* was in attendance, and it was quite the family affair. Michael Hennesey, star of *Beauty*, attended with his wife. He praised the eccentric filmmaker saying, "Jean's the coolest guy I know and a hell of a director." Charlotte Reed also made an appearance with her husband, echoing the sentiments of the night, calling Mercier "an artistic visionary."

One of the biggest surprises came when Rupert Reed arrived arm in arm with his costar Georgia Sinclair Forrester, who proudly showed off an engagement ring. Reed explained he and Forrester "fell madly in love while making the film." The pair couldn't take their eyes off each other, prompting reporters to note that she seemed to be following in her parents' footsteps; they also met on a Mercier set. She said, "Rupert and I would be lucky to have an ounce of the love my parents share." When asked if they were trying to make a public red-carpet splash like her parents famously did at the Cannes Film Festival decades earlier, she was quick to say, "I don't think my parents even noticed anyone else was there. Their eyes only saw each other. Rupert and I feel the same." Reporters congratulated Forrester on the early award buzz for what many are calling her breakout performance. When asked if she hoped to win Oscar gold, she didn't miss a beat, squeezing her fiancé's arm and saying, "I already scored my gold."

In another unexpected turn, for the first time and to the delight of the media and fan gallery, the entire Forrester family walked the red carpet: movie star Finn Forrester and his wife Gabriella Sinclair Forrester, eldest daughter Betty with her beau, and son Albert with his beau. They dazzled the media, posing for photographs. Finn told the press he was "incredibly proud" of daughter Georgia and all his children. The Oscar winner added that it was "important to our family to support Georgia and our dear friend Jean to whom we owe so much." When asked what he and his wife were looking forward to at this stage of their lives, they smiled at each other, and he simply said, "Everything."

But in a twist that no one saw coming, the biggest surprise of the night came from Mercier himself. When a reporter congratulated Mercier on his extraordinary career, the tempestuous director barked, "Save your judgment. I'm still above ground." Asked to clarify if he was coming out of retirement, Mercier announced, "I have written another script. I am in the middle of casting." Speculation immediately began swirling that the cast of *Celebration* would reunite for the project and their appearance on the red carpet was a publicity stunt. When confronted with the rumors, Mercier smirked and said, "Time shall tell. I hope to start shooting late summer. We will see what happens, what fate has in store. I shall die someday not so far off. Until then I shall live. Art never dies. That is our reality, our inescapable truth, our cinematic destiny."

ACKNOWLEDGMENTS

Thank you to the entire team at She Writes Press, especially Brooke Warner, Shannon Green, and Addison Gallegos. I'm incredibly grateful for your unfailing support. I also extend a spirited thank-you to Crystal Patriarche and everyone at BookSparks for helping readers find this book. Thank you to the early reviewers for your generous endorsements. Sincere appreciation to Shalen Lowell, world-class assistant and spiritual bodyguard. Heartfelt thanks to Celine Boyle for your invaluable feedback. Thank you to Anne Durette for the copyediting services. Liza Talusan and the Saturday Writing Team—thank you for building such a supportive community and allowing me to be a part of it. To my social media community and colleagues, thank you boundlessly for your support. My deep gratitude to my friends, especially Vanessa Alssid, Melissa Anyiwo, Sandra Faulkner, Ally Field, Jessica Smartt Gullion, Pamela Martin, Laurel Richardson, Xan Nowakowski, Eve Spangler, and J. E. Sumerau. As always, my love to my family. Madeline Leavy-Rosen, you are my light. Mark Robins, you're the best spouse in the world. Thank you for all that words cannot capture. This book is in loving memory of my teacher, mentor, and friend, Mr. Barry Shuman.

ABOUT THE AUTHOR

PATRICIA LEAVY, PHD, is a best-selling author. She has published over fifty books, earning commercial and critical success in both nonfiction and fiction, and her work has been translated into numerous languages. Over the course of her career, she has also served as series creator and editor for ten book series, and she cofounded *Art/Research International: A Transdisciplinary Journal*. She has received over one hundred book awards. Recently, *After the Red Carpet* won the American Fiction Book Award for Romance. She has also received career awards from the New England Sociological Association, the American Creativity Association, the American Educational Research Association, the International Congress of Qualitative Inquiry, and the National Art Education Association. In 2016, Mogul, a global women's empowerment network, named her an "Influencer." In 2018, the National Women's Hall of Fame honored her, and SUNY New Paltz established the "Patricia Leavy Award for Art and Social Justice." In 2024 the London Arts-Based Research Centre established "The Patricia Leavy Award for Arts-Based Research." Please visit www.patricialeavy.com for more information.

Author photo © Mark D. Robins

Looking for your next great read?

We can help!

Visit www.shewritespress.com/next-read
or scan the QR code below for a list
of our recommended titles.

She Writes Press is an award-winning
independent publishing company founded to
serve women writers everywhere.